ELEVENTH STREET

A Story of Redemption

By Steven K. Bowling

Visit my website at www.StevenKBowling.com or
www.EleventhStreetPublications.com

Printed in the United States of America
First Printing: December 2016
Published by Sojourn Publishing, LLC

ISBN: 978-1-62747-405-4
eBook ISBN: 978-1-62747-012-4

Contents

In memory of my father

"Salute Rufus chosen in the Lord ..." (Romans 16:13).

I.

"A thousand shall fall at thy side, and ten thousand at thy right hand, but it shall not come nigh unto thee" (Psalms 91:7).

1.

Pacific Islands – 1944

"Just one more time, oh Lord, let me make it to shore," he mumbled out loud. As he crouched in the right rear of the Landing Vehicle Tracked ("LVT"), the amphibious landing craft and troop conveyor, Lucas's first order of business was to usher everyone out of the LVT and into the water. As the last to exit, he would be the most vulnerable to a continuous onslaught of targeted mayhem. Men shot or killed in front would be dragged to shore by their fellow soldiers or pushed back inside the conveyor. No time to mourn their wounds or their passing; no time to retaliate against the instigators of their demise. Just live, the primal instinct. Survival, the only thought. Get to shore and find cover. Making it to shore became the most immediate and compelling goal of his life.

"Just let me make it to shore; just one more time," Lucas silently repeated to himself. The troop conveyor rocked and heaved, then rolled upward, and quickly dropped, being thrust and slammed by ocean waves with such force that helmets fell off. Men crouched in the rear of the conveyor braced themselves against each other. Men leaning toward the front stoically waited for the launching gate to fall open, preparing to face the coming barrage of enemy fire.

Sprays of saltwater soaked their gear and dampened their spirit as they bounced through rolling waves. The smells of vomit and the urine of frightened men, mingled with the spray of saltwater and fumes of diesel fuel, created a putrid odor. The LVT rocked with an aroma of fear, a smell of death disguised.

Shells had rained down on the beach since the break of dawn. Amphibious assault had matured to an intense level of complex savagery. And today, Lucas Marcum of Harlan County, Kentucky, would make another landing. He would participate in a methodical, well-planned invasion onto an island held and fortified by the Japanese Imperial Army.

Migrating from Harlan County through Eastern Kentucky to Ohio, Lucas enlisted in the Army. After basic training, he had settled at Pearl Harbor. He was still a young recruit, just barely nineteen years of age in September, 1941. But the innocence of his youth, and the peaceful bliss of that island paradise, were shattered one Sunday morning while he ate breakfast with his brother, Julian, in Schofield Barracks. December 7th was the first time someone had tried to kill Lucas – and Lucas had reciprocated in kind.

Today's landing was just one of many vast endeavors by the Army to regain control of the Pacific Theater. For Lucas, it was much more than an island landing; it was another moment of ultimate truth. He had been in a LVT before. This time, the next few minutes would decide who lived and who died.

Prayers, some audible, most merely whispered, echoed inside the metal container. Soldiers, crammed and huddled together like sardines in a can, waited for the sound of gears and chains to move and open the front gate of the conveyor. The sounds of prayer were muffled by the roar of the diesel engines pushing them to shore, and the thumping of the conveyor's bottom as it bounced on the ocean water beneath them. Both machine and nature vibrated in unison to a rhythm of portending doom.

Though many had knelt before the chaplain on the ship deck just moments ago, the LVT that now carried them to battle became a booth of true confession; a capsule where the sins of a lifetime flashed through their minds. Their prayers rose to a cloudless sky with a common theme: "Oh Lord, forgive me; let me make it to shore."

The sun had been rising as quickly as did the heat. Bountiful rays of light slowly baked Lucas's back. The rock and roll of the helmet scuffed the nape of his neck. First water, then sand and palm trees lay before him, but only if he did not drown while stepping off the LVT. When the LVT hit bottom thirty yards from shore, the entire squad of fifteen men were still in front of him. "Faster. Go faster," Lucas yelled as the men sprang to their feet and jumped into chest-deep water. They carried too much weight on their shoulders. Their backpacks contained enough supplies to last for days. But tomorrow was of no concern. They hoped only for enough ammunition to last the day.

Machine gun fire from the LVT's rear compartment muffled the cries of warriors too young to truly fear what lay ahead. But Lucas knew what lay in store. He had been here before. "Just let me make it to shore, dear God; just one more time is all I ask today."

The battleships had done their best to prepare the way, shelling the island's beach with tons of artillery fire. Their onslaught felled palm trees, shredded the brush, blasted trenches and carved out holes on the beach, some deep enough to hide a jeep. But many of the deadly missiles had overreached the beach, and many palm trees still guarded the shore.

Those trees hid the enemy within, perched high like ravenous birds of prey. The Japanese waited. They patiently waited. Poised like vultures adjusting their position. Peering for live flesh. Finding their target, sharpening their beaks and refining their aim. They were camouflaged to resemble the roost upon which they lay, covered with brush strapped to their backs, an invisible menace to the object of their scorn.

The Japanese army were trained and ferocious killers. Today, they would fight to retain control of the island at all costs. They would fight to the death. There would be no surrender. Their duty to defend had become a holy, sacrificial mission.

Japanese aircraft flew overhead from an airfield further inside the island's imposing barrier to amphibious assault. Army troops approaching the beach were not their immediate target. These planes were attacking the American naval battleships that were lofting artillery shells at their stronghold. These pilots would also fight to the death, intentionally diving their planes onto the decks of the ships they had vowed to destroy.

Men fell in front of Lucas, no longer able to hear or respond to his urgent plea to go faster. Those who were not stopped by bullets, faltered in the deep water. The weight on their shoulders was too heavy; the waves and undercurrent at their feet too strong. They were wading through chest-deep water while under enemy fire. Several men lost their rifles and other essential gear. A bottleneck at the exit ramp of the LVT would give the enemy an opportunity to massacre them all. If the squad failed to reach the beachhead, it would be like shooting fish in a barrel. No hope for escape – and no place to hide.

"Faster, go faster," Lucas screamed until finally he too was at the exit ramp. He jumped into the ocean. The saltwater splashed onto his face, burning and blurring his vision. He raised his knees high to skip and hop through the waves, leaping forward through the water toward shore with all the strength he could muster.

"Just get me to shore, dear Lord; just get me to shore," he cried aloud as he struggled to the beach looking for cover, searching for anything he could get behind or get under to shield himself from the unseen hail of bullets zipping and pinging all around.

As he zigzagged his way onto the beachhead, machine gun fire riveted and sprinkled the sand at his feet. While trying to sidestep and detour the stream of bullets that besieged him, he fell into a divot left by a ship's artillery shell. On his belly, he crawled to the deepest and most protected edge of the crevice and curled up like a baby, seeking fetal comfort in a corner.

His canteen was full of bullet holes and oozing out the last of its water. He had been the last man out of the LTV, and the last to make it to shore. "Thank you Lord," he shouted. "Now get me off this beach."

After what seemed like an eternity of violent thunder, an eerie silence fell upon the beach. No shouts of bravado; no bullets whizzing by; no cries of anguish. His fellow soldiers had either advanced beyond the beachhead and into the jungle or were dead. He could not hear a sound; neither could he see. The divot had become a temporary womb of refuge, a hiding place. Lucas was hidden from not only the enemy, but from his own troops.

Then came the blistering sounds of "zip, zip, zip; ping, ping, ping," all aimed at his feet. Machine gun fire seemed to be directed at Lucas, and not randomly scattered across the beach. These bullets were targeted specifically at him, and from an angle that gave the shooter at least a partial view of his body, now snuggled in the gutted remains of an artillery shell hole.

Lucas furiously kicked at the sand, making piles at his feet. He pawed and clawed more sand with his hands from the front of the hole to enlarge the divot, to make it a bigger and deeper shelter. With bullets still spraying around him, he desperately continued to dig, at times fantasizing that he might dig a tunnel under the beach to safety. But as sand blew into his mouth, the taste of reality returned. It was not yet six in the morning and he was trapped on the beach. He had no water, and at least one Japanese soldier had him in view. Today, this unknown, faceless assailant would devote whatever time it took. First, to make his life miserable; then to end it altogether.

The sun was warm at 10:00 AM. It stood high and hot at noon. Lucas was thirsty. The heat was almost unbearable by 2:00 PM. His throat was parched. In eight hours it seemed as though Lucas had dug a hole wide and deep enough to hide a tank. As long as he lay near the deepest end of the divot facing the jungle, he could not be seen. At least that was what he hoped. He had been digging since sunrise. The heat had drained his energy. His splintered and empty canteen served as a constant reminder of his thirst and the enemy's proximity. Despite the sniper's looming and obvious intent to kill, all Lucas could think about was water. Water to drink. Something to cool his scorched tongue.

"Just one drink of water, dear Lord. Just a few drops would do," he thought. Maybe he had not prayed earnestly enough, but he had made it to the beach unscathed. Why hadn't he prayed for even more protection? Why hadn't he prayed: "Get me off this beach; take me into the jungle with my fellow soldiers"? Better still, why hadn't he prayed: "Let the war be over and take me home"?

He remembered what the preacher, Buck Johnson, had once said, "You have not because you ask not, that's what the Bible says." The preacher was almost family. The preacher's brother had married Lucas's sister. Everyone called the preacher Pastor. Even Lucas, who hadn't been to church in years, called him Pastor.

Whether that was just Pastor talking, or what the Bible really taught, it didn't matter today. Lucas was asking; indeed, he was begging for more than a drink of water. He was praying, sincerely praying, for the first time in his life: "Please, God, show me a way off this beach; dear God, take me home to my family."

"Where is the rain that comes every afternoon? Oh, the rain would be so nice," he thought. Rain would give him a few drops of water, but rain would weaken his manmade sandcastle of refuge. Even worse, rain could fill it with pools of water. Dying from the sun's heat or drowning, which would be worse? Deep inside his soul, he knew that neither would happen today. The sniper's bullet would probably get him first.

The heat continued to bear down upon him, but the ocean breeze sporadically blew a brief respite. Lucas took off his boots and loosened the laces to air them out. Then he took off his socks and spread them flat across the top of each boot, hoping they would dry out more quickly.

Machine gunfire resumed, focusing near his feet at the far end of the hole. With each burst of machine gunfire from the sniper, Lucas continued to dig. This was no modest foxhole. A water buffalo could hide in this crevice. He unstrapped the backpack and slid the supplies and ammunition from his shoulders. He unbuttoned his shirt and carefully maneuvered out of it. He spread out the shirt across the backpack, like his socks, to dry.

Next he rolled up his pant legs and tightened his belt. His pants had been heavy with saltwater and then with sand. His lean and fit one hundred and thirty-pound frame had artificially blossomed to a much heavier weight. Earlier, it felt as if he was wearing a whole load of wet laundry around his waist. But the sun, as it scorched his face and throat, had also baked his trousers dry. It was after four in the afternoon. No fluids since breakfast on the ship. Over twelve hours had passed. No fluids to generate sweat. His skin felt like cold rubber.

Coconut trees had been felled by the dozen on the beach. Coconuts were scattered up and down the shoreline. The bodies of many comrades lay motionless in the sand, body parts scattered near and far. Other bodies were being intermittently washed to and from the beach shore by ocean waves. These men did not make it past the beachhead into the jungle. They had wanted to live as much as Lucas did, and no doubt had prayed as hard as Lucas had. They had family too, maybe a wife and children. Why had Lucas made it this far, and not them?

Lucas made a decision. He would not die in a hole, lying half naked and thirsty. If death was his fate today, the enemy must intervene. The sniper would have to be a better shot than he had been so far.

The intermittent barrage of gunfire into the foxhole served as a constant reminder of his present peril, but it also stirred his curiosity about two completely unrelated things: Where were the rest of his fellow soldiers? And where was the closest coconut?

Each time he peered above the sand, another volley of bullets would be thrust in his direction. Yet, with each quick glance, he could see no one moving on the beach. The soldiers he could see had either drowned or been killed. Who had made it to the cover of the jungle? Was he the only one still alive? Was he the only one still pinned down on the beach, a prisoner trapped in an inverted sand dune? The sun was setting, dusk drawing nigh.

How could he angle himself into position for a clear shot at the sniper? How could he shoot at a man whose exact location was still unknown? Was the assailant lying in brush on the ground or perched in a tree? How far away was this sniper? Was he to the left, to the right or straight ahead? Would he be able to see the sniper in the dark? Would the sniper be able to see him?

The more Lucas pondered and plotted his next move, the thirstier he became. The coconut he saw was not within easy reach. It was at least five yards, maybe six yards away. He had always been quick and a fast runner. Though only five foot six inches tall, he still could have been a high school athlete. He could have played some kind of sport, but he was always changing schools. Moving with his family to greener pastures. Literally moving. Literally, seeking greener pastures. Moving was the norm for a sharecropper, the life and livelihood of his father. Most of the schools he attended didn't even have a ball team, so what the heck. On to the next farm; maybe fertile fields would be found to plow.

Five yards, that's all. He could jump out of the foxhole, dive for the coconut and return with refreshment; lifesaving refreshment. At least he wouldn't die of thirst. If he could hold out until dark, well maybe, just maybe, he could shift himself in the divot for a clear shot at his nemesis. He still had his rifle. The sun would be setting soon. Maybe he could hold out until dark.

"It's just five yards," he thought. "I can do that. I believe I can do that. Five yards to either live or die. Yes, sir," he said to himself. "I can do five yards."

He was already barefoot and unencumbered by the supply pack. His shirt and socks had thoroughly dried by the sun's heat. His boots may have shrunk in size just a bit, but he could stretch them out again. Right now, he didn't need any of those articles of clothing. They would just slow him down. All things considered, the Lord hadn't forsaken him yet. He was on the beach. He was still alive. His pants were dry and. glory be, the Lord had laid a coconut practically at his feet.

That coconut could make the difference. With some fluid in his body, he would be refreshed and energized. He would be ready to greet the darkness and locate his enemy's position. Without something to drink, he would dehydrate, becoming weak and totally vulnerable to the sniper's incessant and sinister interest in his presence on the beach.

Five yards out; five yards back. He counted out loud, "One thousand one, one thousand two ..." Could he do five yards out and back in five seconds?

How much time would the sniper need to take aim, put Lucas in his sight and blast him straight to hell? "Oh, not hell," he thought. "Not hell, dear Lord. Forgive me for everything I've done wrong and if I don't make it back to this hole, take me on to a better place." Then he wondered if Pastor would approve.

Lucas, praying only in a crisis. Praying only when things looked bleak and bad. Had he thanked the Lord for anything today? Should he have said "Amen"?

He scooted as close to the edge of his foxhole as the sniper would grudgingly permit. Rolling his pants legs up even further past his knees, he crouched like a tiger ready to pounce upon its prey. He took a deep breath and leaped from the foxhole, lunging toward the coconut, reaching with both hands extended.

Machine gunfire flayed at his feet as he scooped the coconut up with his right hand and threw it back over his left shoulder toward the foxhole. In one simultaneous and fluid motion, he leaped and dived back into the only shelter he had known all day. The sniper exhausted a belt of machine gun bullets. Trying to kill a man in search of something to eat and drink, all for naught. The bullets spread the sand under his feet, but failed to reach their intended target. One man and one coconut had made a connection. One man had a chance to live yet awhile longer.

Lucas crawled to the high end of his hole and cradled the coconut close to his chest. While catching his breath, he breathed a prayer of thanks. Then he pulled out his knife, eager to feast on the fruit of his labor. As he lifted the coconut for his first drink in hours, a single rifle shot rang out. The rustling of heavy leaves being torn and thick brush crumpling, and then loud thumps bouncing off the ground, were the only sounds he heard.

Silence lingered for what seemed like an eternity. The sun continued to fall from the sky. Shadows of the coconut palms began to form on the beach. The ocean breeze grew stronger. He could hear the waves beating against the shoreline behind him. Then, a fellow soldier shouted out, "I got him, Lucas. You can come out now. The bastard's dead."

"Home," he thought, "home. I may make it back after all."

Going home was his heart's desire, but it wasn't yet an option. Even though Lucas had survived Pearl Harbor, beach landings and hand-to-hand combat in the Dutch New Guinea jungles, along with several smaller skirmishes and today's near-death experience, he had more combat to endure. Leyte would require American and Allied forces to mount the largest amphibious operation of the war in the Pacific. That campaign would cost over 3,500 American lives and leave another 12,000 wounded and disabled. Then, Mindoro and Marinduque Islands awaited.

He would lose his closest friend in a furious battle at Luzon's Zig Zag Pass, and many fellow soldiers would die while making another amphibious landing on Corregidor, fighting under a hot sun, on the well-defended island. He would fight for his life in each encounter. Just live, the primal instinct. Survival, his primary goal.

Within days after the battle at Luzon, Lucas stood behind a crowd of distinguished onlookers. Worn, weary and well off the shoreline, he observed General

Douglas McArthur repeatedly rehearse and stage his famous "I shall return" walk. His uniform clean and pressed, the General did not have to dodge a bullet, confront the enemy or fear drowning in the deep water. He confidently strolled through gentle small ripples of ocean waves onto the safe and secure Philippine shore.

Cameramen rolled the film, doing second and third "takes" until the General was satisfied with the imaging. Newspaper reporters hurriedly wrote the press account for immediate release and worldwide publication. High-level military personnel smiled, applauded and congratulated themselves as though they had personally fired every shot and killed all the enemy. Lucas watched as they staged the whole show. He was physically and emotionally drained.

By the end of the Luzon campaign, Lucas had been part of the most heavily engaged infantry in the United States Army. For most of the men in the Sixth Army, especially Lucas's 24th Division, it would still be months before they returned home. During the last days of the conflict, virtually all were near exhaustion. They had spent over 306 days in combat. The last 219 days had been continuous. The 24th Infantry Division was among the first to see combat in World War II, and among the last to stop fighting.

They had learned to kill. To kill automatically and without hesitation. They had to be reprogramed not to kill. Most especially, not to kill the Japanese. It would take time. They had to get used to the idea of no longer living with a rifle as a constant companion. This would also take time. Many still suffered from malaria and jungle rot, but these ailments would pale in comparison to the memory of combat, and the flashbacks of indescribable horrors. This would take more than time. They would be forever changed by the war, and by the loss of so many friends who had sacrificed their lives at the peak of their youth. They would be changed, most of all, by their own survival.

Lucas would return to San Francisco in August, 1945, and travel by train to Hamilton, Ohio. His sisters and their families had moved there during the war. He would have to learn how to appreciate the simple joys of life. Joy, a distant cousin to peace. Not just an end to war, but a restoration of the inner man, a healing of the soul. This too would take more than time, more than just surviving.

2.

Eastern Kentucky – 1930's

Before the war began, home for Lucas Marcum had been near London, Kentucky. His family had migrated there to rent a farm. He would work the fields and pay the rent by sharing the proceeds of the crops they planted, harvested and sold at market. Sweet corn, green beans, lettuce, beets, radishes, cucumbers and other edible vegetables grew in abundance, but they were not the main source of income. Tobacco was the cash crop, and tobacco plants dominated the plowed and prepared acres of rich, fertile soil of Laurel County. Too many farms in the past had failed. The hard red clay either conquered or choked the precious and costly seed that the Marcum family had spread, or the tender sprouts escaping the soil would be burnt by the heat to unmarketable stubble.

Lucas's mother had died when he was barely eleven years old. The death of his mother became another excuse for his father to drink sour mash and go fox hunting for days and weeks at a time. As Lucas grew older, his father's absences became more frequent and longer in duration.

Upon his return from a long absence, his father often talked about another farm he had seen, a farm that could be repaired and made into a profitable venture. Another farm, greener pastures, a brighter future – these were constant themes for a widowed father with more children than money; more dreams than reality; and more interest in drinking than feeding his family.

Old man Marcum had sired eleven children. Six were now grown and gone, one dead at age two, but four still at home and hungry, including Lucas. The burden seemed greater than he could bear. He never acknowledged that eleven live births, several miscarriages and a constant change of address might have been a contributing factor to his wife's early death. But nothing was his fault. To him, life was a game of chance. As in poker, he had been dealt a bad hand and he could no longer bluff his way out of the game. It was time to gather what chips he had left and find another game, at a different table. He eventually left his family for good.

Lucas had learned how to hang a new door on the shed, mend a fence and plant the crops. Though barely a teenager, he walked and talked like a grown man. There was no chore too heavy or job too big for Lucas. He would tackle the project with gusto, even though he knew little or nothing about it. He only knew that it had to be done, and that his father was not around.

The older brothers helped financially as best they could, but all of the Marcum brothers together couldn't provide enough for themselves and the younger children by farming. They all had part-time jobs and were letting themselves out for hire to do small construction projects for larger, more profitable farms and for local businessmen who had not gone bust in the Depression.

Unlike their father, the Marcum brothers did not quit. They operated under a different set of rules, with principles and values of life gleaned from their uncles and their mother's side of the family. Tight family bonds were their response to harshness and turmoil, and if necessary, violence. Violence was never for economic gain, but over honor. They lived in the hills of Kentucky, where feuds among the hill folk lasted for generations, or until everyone was killed.

They anticipated hard work as a matter of course, and they were not intimidated by the hard red clay of Harlan, or any other county in Eastern Kentucky. They were quick tempered, but inclined to hard work. Too often their labor was followed by boisterous leisure and, to the chagrin of their mother, heavy drinking. They were easy to provoke and quick to fight, especially if family or friends were disparaged. True to their Scotch-Irish heritage, they unwittingly lived out the motto of Scotland: *"Nemo Me Impune Lacessit,"* a Latin phrase that means that "no man cuts me with impunity." They didn't know Latin, but in their own Kentucky backwoods terminology, it meant that if one Marcum got pinched, the whole family flinched. By this code of honor, they defended themselves, family and friends.

Lucas took on some of the responsibilities of a surrogate father for his three younger siblings. Sadie, an older sister, was already married to Hank Johnson, Pastor's brother. Sadie and Hank already had children of their own, but Sadie took on the role of pretending to be her younger siblings' mother as well. Sadie and Hank reared the younger Marcum children, two small girls and a boy. Lucas helped as best he could before he enlisted in the Army.

Sadie was determined that Lucas should finish high school if at all possible. Despite having attended a new school every year for the last five years, Lucas still had enough credits to graduate in the spring if he could only attend class and finish out the year. But the financial pressure on a young man trying to be a surrogate father to his siblings eventually took its toll.

One spring day in 1941, he stepped out of school and into line with his two of his older brothers at the draft board and joined the Army. Lucas, Julian and Marcus would assign the vast majority of their monthly pay to Sadie to help support the younger ones still at home. Hopefully, they could learn a trade in the Army that would benefit them and their family after their enlistment hitch expired. Horace, the oldest Marcum brother, had already joined the Army in 1939 after Hitler invaded Poland. The next oldest sibling, Favor, had been drafted under the Selective Training and Service Act of 1940. By December 7, 1941, five Marcum brothers were in the Army.

During the war, many of their friends and family members moved north to Ohio. There were few steady jobs available in Eastern Kentucky. Buck Johnson, Hank's brother and better known as "Pastor," had already led many of his congregation to Hamilton in the fall of 1939. He had helped them find work in the plants and steel mills.

Sadie and Hank followed after all the adult Marcum brothers were in the Army, but they did not abandon the younger Marcum sisters and brother. Hank was basically a kind and understanding man, and more than willing to take them into their new home. But his kindness and understanding was massaged by the fact that Lucas, Julian and Marcus sent most of their military pay back to Sadie to help defray the cost of rearing three who were not his own. It also provided some extra cash to invest in properties abandoned during the Depression, or foreclosed upon by the bank.

Though Hank Johnson was kind, he was also an insightful businessman. No one got the best of him in a trade or business transaction, and no one lived in his house for free, even if the stay was being subsidized by the U.S. Army. Sadie's siblings were put to work. The two younger sisters did laundry for the disabled or the homebound. They mowed yards for the neighbor whose son had been drafted, or helped fix up a house for rental.

Hank was also a city farmer, with cows, pigs and mules on vacant acreage across town. The animals needed to be fed and tended to, neither of which Hank had time to do himself. The youngest Marcum brother, still not a teenager, was assigned the task of caring for the livestock and performing the chores that a farm required. No job was left unattended. If Sadie's younger siblings could walk, talk and eat, in Hank's mind, they could also work.

While in high school, Lucas met Margaret Gibbs. Maggie was the nickname her friends and family called her. She was the youngest of fourteen children, with ten sisters and three brothers. Raised on a nearby farm, Maggie knew firsthand the hardships of squeezing a livelihood out of the ground and the hazards of having too many mouths to feed. Not only did Lucas and Maggie have a common background, they both had absentee fathers.

Lucas's father had physically abandoned his family, ostensibly in search of greener pastures. Maggie's father had journeyed into the private world of his own mind, an emotionless existence. The economic downturn had repressed and depressed his spirit to the point that he was virtually an invalid. He seldom ventured out of the house. He rarely spoke.

Maggie was searching for a father figure, and Lucas had lost his mother years ago. The chemistry between them was clearly evident. For weeks they had made visual assessments of each other, grunting a quick "hello" or "how you doing" while passing each other in the school hallway. Eventually, they stopped for brief conversations between classes, and met to say goodbye after school in the courtyard.

Both of them had chores to do at home, and neither could linger after school. Maggie rode home with a neighbor. Lucas walked home alone. Their time together was always brief, fleeting and interrupted. Neither one had the courage to arrange an opportunity to meet outside of school. That is, until one Friday afternoon.

Flirting from a distance and trying to get his attention, Maggie threw a broken broom handle in Lucas's direction down the hallway at school. Trying to be cute and seductive, she nearly committed murder.

The broom handle struck Lucas in the forehead. He fell backwards against the wall lined with school lockers and slid down to a sitting position, nearly unconscious. Maggie was horrified, then embarrassed if not ashamed. Only Maggie's girlfriends laughed, but when they saw blood dripping down Lucas's face, they shrieked in terror. Boys close by knelt down to determine whether Lucas was still alive. If he was still alive, was he breathing, and was there anything they could do to help?

To everyone's relief, Lucas opened his eyes and sheepishly smiled. He was alive and, remarkably, in good spirits. He slowly regained his vision and stood up with the help of two schoolmates. He held a handkerchief over the wound in his forehead and looked toward Maggie. She was still standing several feet away, frozen in fear.

"Want to go to the camp meeting tonight? A little dose of some old-time religion might help your aim!" he said in Maggie's direction, his voice still unstable.

"Only if my sister chaperones," she replied. "I wouldn't want anyone to think I was out alone, especially with you. They might think you'd been hit with a broomstick!"

3.

Pastor – 1939

Buck Johnson had been preaching every night for the last five days. The camp meeting had been a huge success. It would be his last outdoor revival in Laurel County. It was springtime, in April, 1939. He had announced his intention to move north to Ohio. The crowd was huge. Seemed like everyone in the county wanted to hear him preach at least one more time.

People traveled by the wagonload, by horseback and by foot to hear him preach. The warmth of spring and the cool evening breeze contributed to everyone's physical comfort during the services. Buck, Pastor Buck or simply "Pastor," as he was known, took great pleasure in making the unrepentant and reprobate as uncomfortable as possible.

Pastor was an imposing figure. Standing well over six feet, he was taller than most men in the county. Despite his fifty-two years, his broad shoulders and thick arms still bore evidence of his physical strength and stamina. With his shirtsleeves rolled up past his elbows, the well-formed muscles of his arms rippled with each movement of his arms. When he lifted the Bible with one hand, you could see the size of his enormous fist. Everyone knew that he meant business when he slammed the pulpit with his other hand while warning the audience that hell was real. His hair was a light gray, almost white, and worn with a longer cut than most men his age. The ends curled up slightly just above his collar. He had the face of a warrior: tough, intense, with sharp-edged cheekbones. His blue eyes were like a flame of fire. At night, with lanterns burning on each side of the makeshift pulpit, one could imagine that a gray-haired Samson was in your midst.

He might have been a young Samson in his youth. Born in the same year as the famous Alvin York of Fentress County, Tennessee, Pastor also had served in World War I. Unlike Sergeant York, who received many medals for valor, including the Congressional Medal of Honor, Pastor had not killed a single German soldier. He never even left the States, and no movie had been made about his life. But in the eyes of his friends and neighbors, he was still a hero.

Since the end of the "war to end all wars," Pastor had devoted himself to changing the world for better. Just as Alvin York had been reformed from a hard-drinking and rowdy-living scoundrel into a man known as the "Singing Elder," Pastor had also been transformed. He was now a just and upright man. Many called him the "Shouting Preacher."

Pastor had no formal training as a minister. He had no high school diploma. He would not have been admitted to a seminary, even if he had applied. The Baptist seminary in Louisville required a college degree. He had no books other than the Bible, and he had only one good suit, two dress shirts and a handful of hand-me-down ties. His shoes were old and worn, and in need a good polish and shine.

Pastor would not have been accepted to a seminary by the admissions staff. Other men searching for credentials and badges of divinity would have kept their distance. He lacked the manners and charm to become a professionally trained minister. He lacked the capacity or even the will to be either mannered or charming.

Pastor was a man from the backwoods of Kentucky. His neighbors gathered to him because he loved and cared for them, and they knew it. They met in a primitive church house. They worshipped God within the framework of their literal theological views. They were not ashamed to give free rein to their emotions. Pastor had been raised up to be their minister, and no special training was required. He had been called by God Himself to preach, and he did not need the refinements offered at the seminary. Pastor expressed the views and hopes of his people. He was at one with his flock.

Pastor may have lacked a formal education, but he could read with understanding and had nearly a photographic memory. When he preached, it was as though God's power attended every word. People in attendance often fell or convulsed as they cried out for mercy. At times, he appeared to be a flaming zealot, shouting out loud, thunderous gusts of warning. At other times, he was meek, with a gentle and humble voice, whispering words of compassion, encouragement and hope. Pastor did not need a degree to preach or persuade. The good Lord Himself had fully equipped this man for the task at hand.

Lucas and Maggie sat in the back row of folding chairs. They were just barely outside the funeral-home tent that Pastor had borrowed for the revival. They sat attentively as Pastor preached one of his more tender sermons on love and devotion to family.

Too many men had lost their jobs during the Depression, then their hope. Many wives and children bore deeper emotional scars than hunger pains because of the despair that had come over their husbands and fathers. Their breadwinner had been on a losing streak too long, and was about to quit altogether, if he had not already done so.

Pastor begged the men to call upon the Lord. He promised that God would renew their strength, and as he quoted scripture to those gathered, he said, "They shall mount up with wings like eagles; they shall run, and not be weary; and they shall walk and not faint."

Pastor continued quoting the Bible, adlibbing a bit as he went along, "Have you not heard? Don't you know? Our God, the Lord and creator of the heavens and the Earth, He doesn't faint and He's not weary. He stands ready and willing to lift you up if you will only humble yourself tonight and ask, simply ask. Brothers and sisters, tonight is the night. Seek Him now! Seek Him while He can yet be found."

Maggie stirred ever so delicately in her seat and leaned over to Lucas with a question. She softly whispered, "Lucas, have you been saved?"

Lucas had never been asked that question so directly, or up so close, except by Pastor. Pastor was his brother-in-law, and he seldom missed an opportunity to box Lucas into a spiritual corner. Lucas deftly avoided Pastor as much as family relations would permit. Obviously, he had heard the question before. He wasn't an outright heathen.

The question was normally asked from a pulpit, and at a distance. He knew what the question was intended to elicit. It was directed to the heart, to the soul. It was seeking an answer to the here and now. Was there joy unspeakable and full of glory in his heart? It was also seeking an answer to his eternal destination. Would he have life after death? Would that life be one of comfort, or of torment?

He had never given Pastor a straightforward answer, and he thought about giving Maggie a sarcastic reply, like "Saved from what?" But he sensed that Maggie was not in a sarcastic or humorous mood. Maggie was serious. She was up close and personal. She was intent on finding out if Lucas was a God-fearing man or a hellion.

She wanted to know about his soul, about his eternal destination. By implication, Maggie was making a preliminary inquiry as to his fitness to be a husband, perhaps even a father. Lucas stiffened, then turned to Maggie and said, "I haven't quit on my family. I never will. Let's go for a walk."

Before the night was over, Lucas knew that he'd have to get some religion before Maggie would ever get serious with him. At the very least, he'd have to promise to go to church every now and then. He hoped that Maggie would wait, because tonight was not the night. Oh no, not tonight.

Lucas would not be graduating from high school. Pastor was leaving for Ohio. Sadie, Hank and what was left of the Marcum family in Kentucky would soon follow. They were all leaving the farm, heading to the city lights. Lucas would move in a different direction. He would enlist in the Army. He wasn't quitting on his family. He was going to find a better way to help.

4.

The Hamilton Migration – 1940s

The Depression was over and the war won, but it was not the best of times. Work was still hard to find. Not that long ago, young boys had left school to work in the fields. Older boys had simply walked out of school and stepped into line at the local draft board. Education was what they learned at home or in the fields or in the service. Their life lessons were not found in school books or in the city libraries or on the chalkboards of a classroom just barely within walking distance from home.

They wanted a better life, but they needed a job. They wanted a family and needed a way to support them. They needed self-esteem. They needed a purpose greater than simply that of survival. The hard life of growing up poor, then seeing men die at their own hand in war did not seem to destroy their zest for life, but it did quiet it. They seldom talked about the war, but the effects were readily apparent. Some were still yellow from malaria-infested jungles, or shell shocked from constant bombardments. They had learned one thing for sure. Life was short and Pastor was right. Hell was real. They had seen and experienced it firsthand.

In Kentucky, the word was out, "There are jobs up north." Plants once filled with war-making equipment were being converted and refitted from building tanks, jeeps and planes into machines designed to meld iron; and fabricate, cut and glean steel for automobiles, refrigerators, and other domestic and industrial uses. The factories stretched from Cincinnati to Hamilton, on to Dayton and all the way north to Detroit and Flint. There was work, and the factories needed workers, no high school or college diploma required. There were good wages available by the hour, and a payday every Friday. You could even take Saturday and Sunday off. Working on weekends paid overtime, but only if you wanted to work.

Some likened their journey north to the Hebrew pilgrimage. Leaving the brick pits of Kentucky, they followed a cloud by day and a pillar of fire by night. They crossed over a muddy, red-tinted Ohio River, hoping to find the Promised Land of their dreams. They never realized that they too, like the Israelites, were entering a wilderness of trials and temptations. The Promised Land was still not in sight. Would it take forty years of wandering to find their dream?

For some, the wilderness journey overwhelmed them. The fire by night was snuffed out. For others, the cloud by day settled in a mist of despair. But for those who did not fear the giants of the land, for those who lifted up their loincloth in hope, they saw and touched the dream. They struggled, but they endured to the end. For those who did endure, it took the help of family, friends and the Lord. It was in church where they found all three.

Pastor had led his flock north out of Kentucky just as surely as Moses had led the Israelites out of Egypt, and he did it before the war had started for America. At that time, the factories were bustling and steel mills glowing hot in southwestern Ohio. By the late 1930s, the factories were churning out tanks, jeeps and planes. They were manufacturing rifles, huge guns and all sorts of armaments.

Officially, these armaments were being made to help England ward off the bombardments of Germany under the Lend-Lease legislation. America was not yet at war, and nobody wanted to innocently start a fight with Hitler. War or no war, the economic boom made jobs available and inspired people to seek them out.

Pastor sold all that he had. He closed his general store in London, Kentucky and set up shop in Hamilton, Ohio. He got the blessing of the Hazel Green Baptist Church of London, Kentucky to organize a new church. The Baptists call it an "arm." With this missionary authority, he opened the doors for the Lord's business on the very same day that Hitler invaded Poland. He named it the First Fellowship Baptist Church of Hamilton. Baptists always want to be the "first." No one ever heard of the "second" Baptist church.

He rented an abandoned office building in the Five Points area, bought used pews and built his own pulpit. He began to preach each Saturday night, Sunday morning and Sunday night. His brother Hank Johnson, Sadie's husband and Lucas's brother-in-law, took over the financial affairs of the church. Pastor looked over the spiritual. As more and more people migrated from Kentucky to Hamilton, the church congregation grew. Even before the war ended, the number attending the First Fellowship Baptist Church exceeded the space available. Pastor began a search for larger accommodations.

With Hank's business acumen and Pastor's power of persuasion, an unlikely site was found. No one in their right mind would have moved a church to the location they selected. But Baptists, especially those from Eastern Kentucky, were often accused of being out of their mind. Being crazy had its benefits, and perhaps for that reason, the price was extremely attractive and affordable.

II.

"If thou doest well, shalt thou not be accepted? And if thou doest not well, sin lieth at the door."

(Genesis 4:7)

5.

East Side Dance Hall – 1944

It had been a hot, muggy Saturday night. The front door gently opened to what previously had been the East Side Dance Hall on Eleventh Street. The people inside meandered down the steps to the sidewalk to visit, chat and laugh with each other. Handshakes, goodbyes and hugs signaled their departure. Some walked to their cars, others walked home. Pastor had dismissed the church service early. The Saturday night fights were being broadcast on the radio. Pastor loved a good prizefight.

The dance hall was awkwardly situated amidst a quiet and rundown residential neighborhood. None of the neighbors could remember when it was built. It had been there when they arrived. The loud dance music and the violent history of the dance hall were in stark contrast to the soft singing and gentle spirit that now filled the building. The neighbors could finally rest peacefully in their homes at night, without aggravation or fear that a fight on the front steps or in the adjacent lot would break out.

Cold beer, hundred-proof liquor and scantily clad women triggered a lot of anger and jealousy. Refreshing their reservoir of self-confidence with strong drink, while repressing the memory of rejection, men competed with each other for the attention of a dance partner, a woman who seemingly became more beautiful with each succeeding drink. Fights often broke out and the police would be called to intervene.

This pattern repeated itself each Saturday night until the murder – a murder in plain view of anyone looking out of the window of their home. A murder on the front steps of a dance hall. It happened so quickly. A young man was viciously stabbed in the stomach. The knife had been rotated and levered so as to nearly gut the man of his intestines. As he fell toward the front door, his throat was slit so savagely that he was nearly decapitated. Gutted and nearly beheaded, the young man would have had his last words, if any, muffled by the blood gushing from his throat and mouth.

No one had heard a scream or a cry for help. The loud music and people talking inside probably drowned out the sound of any plea for mercy or assistance. The murder sparked a neighborhood outcry, and city officials finally closed the dance hall down. No more dancing on Saturday night at Eleventh Street.

The murder had been a front-page headline in the Hamilton Journal for days. "Suspect Still at Large" was the final headline weeks later. Witnesses said that it happened so quickly they didn't see a face. They never heard a scream or even know the man had been stabbed until they saw the blood spreading into a small, sticky pool around his body. The victim had last been seen dancing with a woman inside. He had walked out the front door alone – said he needed some fresh air or a smoke, they couldn't remember. It was the last time he was seen alive.

The detectives interviewed more people and tried to reconstruct the crime scene. They learned that no one in the dance hall had a motive to hurt the victim, let alone kill him. No one had ever seen him before, or even knew his name. They did remember that he was a good dancer, and that he seemed to be focused on just one woman. She too was a good dancer, and a mystery.

Chaos erupted after someone stumbled over the victim's body outside the dance hall. Descriptions of the mystery woman varied to such a degree that the detectives had no solid clue as to who this woman might be.

It had been after midnight when the murder occurred. It was dark. Only one light bulb over the front porch revealed the horror. Which had come first? The wound in the stomach or the slashing of the throat? Blood splatter was on the door frame. A trail of blood led from the porch to the sidewalk and disappeared in a vacant lot to the right of the building. Someone did recall a person standing near the alley to the left of the building as they had entered, but that sighting had been at least an hour before the victim had been found.

The next morning, police inspected the vacant lot next door and meandered back through the neighborhood toward the railroad tracks. During their trek, they found goggles, one heavy-duty work glove and a handmade stiletto. The knife's handle was wrapped with burlap cloth. Its blade was over four inches in length and thick, with a jagged edge, razor sharp. No fingerprints. There was blood on the knife, probably the victim's, but no way to prove to whom it belonged. DNA and forensic testing were not yet available. These were the only clues to a crime that was never solved.

Within weeks, the city closed the dance hall. "A menace to society," the Mayor said. The contents of the building were auctioned, the doors and windows boarded shut. Signs with large letters reading "Do not enter" and "Trespassers will be prosecuted" were posted both in the front and back of the dance hall. The building stood empty and quiet. No more Saturday night revelry.

The only sounds near the site were made by hand-pushed lawnmowers. Neighbors also cut the grass in the vacant lot next door. They were trying to do something wholesome. They were making an attempt to restore a measure of decency, if not sanity, to the city block they called home.

The goggles, work glove and handmade knife were locked in the evidence room at the police station. The victim would later be identified and released to a distant relative for burial. No one attended the funeral. Passersby on the street were drafted to help carry the cheap pine casket to the hearse for transport to a pauper's grave. Several blocks away and further east, the cemetery rested on poorhouse hill, high above the downtown city lights – the place where indigent and homeless strangers were unceremoniously interred.

Was the victim the target of a jealous husband, or was he killed by a turncoat partner in some previously committed crime? Hamilton had a reputation for harboring fugitives from justice. Criminals on the lam from gambling houses in Indianapolis had to drive less than seventy-five miles to escape a raid by the Indiana State police. Thugs from other large cities, including close-by Cincinnati, regularly hid out in Hamilton.

Hamilton had been nicknamed "Little Chicago" in the 1930s for its ruthless and violent reputation. Question upon question were raised by the police and the detectives, but no verifiable answers were ever found. As in so many cases before, the authorities could only be sure of two things, one factual and one maternal: The victim was in the wrong place at the wrong time, and nothing good ever happens after midnight.

Who could have guessed that this den of iniquity would be transformed into a safe place of worship and a fortress of refuge for the downtrodden, ordained as a building favored and blessed of God – a spiritual Beulah Land on Hamilton's east side? Hank Johnson did, and so did his brother, Pastor.

They bought the site at a public tax sale. No one else wanted to bid. No one else dared to risk their reputation. Three years of delinquent property taxes was the price. The transaction was all cash. The money was paid to the City of Hamilton and Butler County in exchange for clear title. The deed of conveyance was made out to the Trustees of the First Fellowship Baptist Church, soon to be renamed as "Eleventh Street Baptist Church." Pastor was now located and doing God's business at 555 Eleventh Street, Hamilton, Ohio.

6.

Preparation for a Journey – 1933

Harold Graber was a determined young man. He had a slight limp; one leg was thin and shriveled, slightly shorter than the other. Not too noticeable when he was dressed, but enough to keep him out of the Army in 1933. He had been one of the first from Kentucky to go to Hamilton. He was settled, and with a job, before the War, many years before Pastor had led his flock north in 1939.

Harold was also small in stature, hardly five feet tall. Since childhood, he had been called "Shorty," a nickname he seemingly did not resent. Shorty Graber was a man with whom you could talk freely and confide in. He was a man who would listen to your troubles. He had experience with trouble. He was a man who had good advice.

Shorty was also very smart. He read well and comprehended what he read. Being short in stature and with a gimpy leg, he wasn't able to run and play with other children in his youth. He loved sports, but couldn't participate. So he read and read. He read old encyclopedias, dictionaries, worn-out text books from school, histories, literature and poems. He read everything he could get his hands on. And most of all, he read the Bible. He truly enjoyed reading the Bible and memorizing verses.

He studied the history of the Bible and how it overlapped into secular history. The Babylonians, the Persians, the Greeks and the Romans were both secular and Biblical reading. He especially enjoyed reading about the Israelites during the time of Christ. Shorty knew more about scripture than anyone he was around. But he never made you feel that he knew more than you. He would ask you questions and lead you to the right answer. Shorty always spoke in a quiet and dignified manner, with excellent diction.

His conduct, at least in public, appeared to be upright and wholesome. But that was his public persona. In the shadows or at night, temptation would often tug on his spiritual sleeve. In his youth, the veil of righteousness, when pulled too hard, tended to fall below his belt.

He had been born in Whitley County, Kentucky, near Corbin. In addition to his books, he had learned some important life lessons. One of these he would never forget. A lesson in his senior year of high school would haunt him to the grave.

Shirley Gresham had not only caught Shorty's eye, but had taken prisoner his heart, soul and body. Shorty thought of her constantly. His stomach ached. His body stirred with passion. He daydreamed that Shirley could be his soulmate for a lifetime of marital bliss. She was quiet, demure and beautiful. He longed for her as she glided down the hallway of school, carrying her books seductively with both hands as she caressed them against her bosom. Her swagger and the movement of her hips mesmerized Shorty as he gazed from a safe distance behind her.

"I'm crazy," Shorty thought to himself, "She'll never look my way." But Shirley had recently looked his way, often catching him in the act of mental lust, only to politely smile and walk away. That is, until Shirley's best girlfriend convinced Shorty to ask Shirley for a date.

"Oh she wants to have some time with you, Shorty. You're so different from the other boys; more mature. And don't you tell her I repeated this, but she thinks you are so very handsome, too!"

Looking back on it all, Shorty should have realized that he was being set up. He was the fall guy. He was the stooge. He was being seduced to do what no other boy in the school would ever dare. The other boys knew better. The other boys were more aware of their surroundings, especially romantic breakups, tears in the hall, talk on the schoolyard. They took notice of relationships. The drama between boys and girls was excellent material for hallway and locker gossip. Shorty focused on his studies, reading and memorizing historical facts. He was oblivious to current events, except to fantasize about a chance to be included.

Shorty did ask Shirley out, and indeed, she agreed. With only a few weeks of school remaining, Shirley managed to dominate Shorty's time between classes and after the school day ended. Long walks home, holding hands, gazing into each other's eyes – and soon, much too soon, they were hugging, then groping at each other, touching and feeling in areas that should have been held in reserve. But she said that she loved him and Shorty didn't know the difference between love and raw animal passion.

Shorty had only dreamed about it, and he had no idea how to actually consummate the opportunity that lay before him. But Shirley knew, and she guided him to a sacred place, encouraging him to stay there and not to worry.

The guilt that fell over Shorty was heavy, like a wet blanket that wrapped around him from head to toe. In the days that passed, Shorty's mind concluded that marriage was the only honorable solution to his guilt and shame. It was the only honorable course of action to preserve Shirley's reputation. Yet despite the feelings of despair that hovered over him in every waking hour, he could not stop thinking about his new experience, and about how he wanted more. Shirley must have felt the same way, because their walks home after school seemed to take a longer and more circuitous route each day.

Their conversation soon took a more serious tone. She said that Shorty had been the first and only man she had loved in that way. Shirley had certainly been the first for Shorty. That fact was the only thing he could be absolutely sure of.

Shirley had been a popular girl at school, and had been the steady girlfriend of at least two boys that Shorty could remember. On more than one occasion, Shorty had seen her crying in the hallway, leaning against the lockers, as she spoke with her most recent boyfriend. At times it looked as though she were pleading with him not to be angry, not to leave her. Shorty wondered, then worried, then wept.

When Shirley told him that she was pregnant, Shorty's knees almost buckled. "Are you sure?" he asked as Shirley's eyes teared and her head slumped forward, resting against Shorty's chest.

"You don't love me," she said. "You lied to me and took advantage of me; and now you're going to walk away and leave me to raise our child, our child, Shorty, to raise it all alone." The volume of her voice rose with each accusation and the bitterness in her face startled Shorty into a quick and emotional response.

"We'll get married; as soon as you can plan it. We'll get married and no one will ever know. I'll get a job. We can find a place of our own. Don't cry, Shirley. We can make this work. Please don't cry."

As the next few days passed, Shorty began to wonder and question his relationship with Shirley in a more calculated manner. They had been together barely five weeks. She'd had two previous boyfriends. She had broken up with a very jealous boy right before she started seeing Shorty. He was also big, and mean, and a spitter. Always spitting, especially when he was angry.

Yes, Shorty had known Shirley, in the Biblical sense, on more than one occasion over the past several weeks, but he could not reconcile the aftermath of his first experience. His experience did not remotely resemble the stories he had heard, all of which were replete with painfully graphic detail. And why had she been crying at the locker that day when her boyfriend seemed to be so cold and distant to her? They had been a couple. They had been together for over a year.

The marriage ceremony was conducted by the Justice of the Peace in his office near the town square. Shirley miscarried within weeks, and left Shorty for another man within months. He had been set up as the fall guy. He had been a stooge; the putative father of another man's child.

Shorty had briefly forsaken all the truths and convictions he held so dear for a temporal and fleeting physical pleasure. He vowed to never be seduced again. He also vowed to leave town as soon as he could. He tried to join the Army, but the Army would not take him. So, he made his way a little further south and east to Pineville. He made plans to attend the Mountain Preachers Bible School. He would repent, do his penitence and try to help others avoid the temptations to which he had fallen prey.

Shorty packed his clothes in a cardboard suitcase. He laid his Bible inside, on top of his shirts. His second-hand suits were in excellent condition. Shorty could sew, replace buttons, mend and patch. While the other children played outside, Shorty had mastered the skills of a domestic servant. He was a meticulous dresser. His shoes were always clean, polished and shined. His shirts were pressed, with seldom a wrinkle or a button out of place. He always caressed his neckties into a perfect Windsor knot. His hair was cut to average length, not too long, not too close to the scalp. It was parted slightly to the left and kept in perfect place by Wildroot Cream Oil.

He caught the bus just outside of Corbin and traveled Highway 25 east and south through Barboursville and other small outposts. The bus lumbered over Clinch Mountain and coasted down toward Pineville, where he saw a huge boulder hanging from the side of a mountain. Chains had been wrapped around the gigantic rock to keep it from falling. It had become somewhat of a tourist attraction.

The Mountain Preachers Bible School had been organized by the native preachers of Bell County, Kentucky in the 1920's. They named it. It sprang from within. They shared a common background and a vision for their region. The great mountain section of Eastern Kentucky was composed of thirty-two counties, all in need of being evangelized. Government statistics at the time indicated that less than eighteen percent of the population professed to be Christian, and that included all denominations and cults. In the opinion of the Preachers School, not being a Baptist was almost the same as being in a cult. The area was served by fewer than one hundred ordained Baptist preachers, and only two had as much as a high school diploma. In their view, the fundamental problem was a lack of Christian leadership – specifically, Baptist leadership.

The organizers solicited the financial help of businessmen in Pineville and Middlesboro. They acquired over three hundred acres of land. The property would be used as an assembly ground for religious education and wholesome recreation. They built frame dormitories and five cabins on the property, and opened the doors in 1924. They paid a mountain preacher $50 a month for six months to contact the Baptist preachers in Bell County and induce them to come to the Preachers Bible School for two weeks of Bible study. At first, only ten agreed to come for a two-week Bible study program. Within a few years, Bible studies were held for five weeks every year. Eventually, enrollment grew to over one hundred mountain preachers. Classes were held all year long.

Enrollment was not yet at its peak when Shorty decided to attend in the fall of 1933. There were only twenty-five students on the campus. He had not been personally invited by anyone to visit and had not told anyone of his intentions to enroll. He was not even certain that he would be admitted. Even though he had a high school diploma and a better-than-average knowledge of the Bible, he hadn't been "called" to preach, and he certainly had not been ordained to preach.

If anyone knew or found out about his failed marital experience, he had no doubt that his admission would be denied. Baptist doctrine frowned on divorce, and absolutely barred anyone who had been divorced from the pulpit. Forgiveness was available to all, even to those who had flagrantly and publicly sinned. You could be a liar, a thief, a cheat, a drunkard, even a womanizer, and still be or become an ordained preacher. With a divorce, you might get forgiveness, but you forever carried the mark of Cain. You were demoted to a second-class Christian, wandering in the land of Nod. The mark of Cain was an automatic disqualification for a preacher. It was a Biblical truth. Even if the "truth" was not actually Biblical, it was certainly Baptist. So, he lied.

Shorty studied diligently. He excelled in test scores on the books of Romans, 1st and 2nd Corinthians and the other Epistles. He did well in the English and grammar classes and faithfully did all his assignments in Old Testament studies. The instructors felt sure that Shorty would soon be called to preach. His teachers knew the reservations Shorty expressed about the ministry, but hoped they would soon dissipate. He would overcome all doubts and fears. They were confident.

He had the look of a preacher; he talked like a preacher. He just might be the most gifted graduate of the school. But Shorty had not walked the walk. He had strayed from the straight and narrow. He knew the truth about himself and was still wrestling with how to avenge it. If the school knew what he knew, they would ask him to leave the school grounds immediately. So, he continued to lie.

Twenty-five students were at the Preachers School, but only five were there full time. All of the men had families. All had to work to support them – all, that is, except Shorty, and one very inquisitive fellow student named John Harkness. Harkness was single and rich. Local businessmen made part-time jobs available, and when school was not in session, work was always available further east toward Harlan in the coal mines. Shorty worked part time in a dry goods store. Farming and mining coal were dirty jobs. John Harkness didn't have to work, but he served as a courier for a law firm in Pineville. He was curious, and he had connections.

John Harkness came from a privileged family. He had access to money, and resources far beyond those of his fellow students. With three years of college on his resume, he had applied and been accepted to the Southern Baptist Seminary at Louisville. The seminary normally required a college degree, but the Harkness family had influence. He had walked among the elite in Baptist circles, and sat in the classroom of some of the greatest Bible scholars of his time. His family had mapped out the road to success and fame for him in the ministry. Every opportunity had been laid at his feet. Yet, with the casualness that often accompanies the privileged, he let it all slip away.

Realizing that he would fail his course work in his second semester, he withdrew from the Louisville seminary. He thought about returning to the state university, but after a brief recovery from his feigned health issues, he tried the ministry again. This time, he would enroll at a school with a curriculum he thought he could master. He could be around people who would look up to him, and admire his past endeavors and pedigree. Harkness wanted to be in front of an audience. He loved to talk and be heard. And there was no greater place to stand and talk to a captive group of people than in a pulpit.

He became incessantly curious about Shorty. Who was this small man, and what was his story? How did he dress so well without the trappings of wealth? Where did he gain the knowledge he so freely gave to all who asked? What was it about this man that everyone so admired? Where was Harold Graber from, and to whom did he owe his good fortune?

Harkness knew that he owed his family more than he could ever repay. That by himself, and on his own merit, he would have never been admitted to the state university, let alone the seminary in Louisville. These and a hundred more questions whirled through Harkness's mind. He was more than curious, he was jealous. Jealous of a cripple.

He spent his spare time looking through records at the Bell County courthouse, searching for deeds or probated wills or other documents of public record. Did Shorty own property? Had he received an inheritance?

When school was not in session, Harkness even searched the public records in nearby Harlan, Leslie and Clay Counties. Shorty's quiet and reserved demeanor served to arouse Harkness's interest and suspicion even more. He was convinced that Shorty had something to hide. Harkness often quizzed Shorty about his past, and his goals for the future. Shorty was always pleasant but vague in his responses, especially to certain questions.

Shorty had lied on his admission forms, and in 1933, Harkness had no way to uncover the truth except through trial and error. Harkness endured many trials and made many errors. Harkness was looking in all the wrong places. He wasn't as smart as he thought.

Shorty left Pineville and the Mountain Preachers Bible School before classes ended, and days before the graduation ceremony. Each graduate would be expected to give a brief sermon, or talk about their plans for the ministry, before leaving the stage. Only nine were scheduled to graduate, and each would be allotted just five minutes to speak.

Shorty could not bear the thought of publicly professing a hope he knew would never materialize. He packed his suitcase again, and caught the early-morning L&N train north to Corbin. He changed trains and railed through London to Cincinnati, and on to Hamilton, Ohio.

Shorty never knew if his absence was noted by the faculty or his fellow students. But one student did notice his absence. John Harkness would never forget the hesitation and reservation Shorty often exhibited on certain Biblical subjects, especially those involving marriage and divorce. He sensed more than reservation; he smelled a spiritual rat. He was convinced that Shorty had something to hide – a secret he would one day expose.

Shorty followed his two older brothers to Ohio. Both had moved to Hamilton, they had good jobs, and they extended a warm welcome to Shorty for a fresh start at life. He got a job as an apprentice welder with Black & Company, and quickly learned the nuances of the trade. As a welder, he got paid more than the average worker in the paper plants and car factories. People said he was the best welder in town. They said he could "weld anything from the crack of dawn to a broken heart."

He lived in a second-floor apartment above a neighborhood grocery and dry goods store, another business with which he was familiar. Working weekdays at Black & Company, he began working Saturdays for his landlord in the ground-floor grocery store. It was there that he met Lyda, the landlord's daughter, and manager of the store's daily activities. Lyda seemed to sense Shorty's feelings of inadequacy and low self-esteem. At first, she attributed his demeanor to loneliness, being a stranger in a new setting. Lyda went out of her way to make Shorty feel wanted and welcome, and would often praise him for his handiwork and attention to detail.

She also observed the difficulty Shorty encountered as he climbed the ladder in the store. The ladder was strapped vertically to the wall and attached to rollers. The ladder would slide the entire width of the wall. It was an essential piece of equipment to reach the dry goods placed on the higher shelves, and still permit a lateral move to either side while remaining on the ladder. While stocking or retrieving items, the climber never had to get off the ladder to relocate or reposition for the next task. Just pull and push, slide from side to side. At times, one leg seemed different than the other, but Shorty's gait appeared normal on level ground. It didn't matter to Lyda.

She also marveled at his skill as a welder. He made small tools: knives, wedges, scissors, screwdrivers, braces and hinges, on his lunch hour. He used scrap metal and slips of discarded iron at work. He brought them to his apartment above the store. He had arranged a small workstation on the back porch, where he molded and ground them into many uses. He gave some of them to Lyda. The grocery was always in need of small tools and minor repairs.

Shorty was quiet, and somewhat secretive. He spent nights alone either reading in his room, or out walking on the streets of Hamilton. He often wandered blocks away from the grocery, stopping in a restaurant for supper or the Lane Public Library for a book. On occasion, he would be tempted to venture further away from his apartment. The distance was not measured by blocks alone, but by his resistance to temptation. Shorty was a lonely man looking for company – company that would not follow him home.

Shorty and Lyda got to know each other as fellow workers and friends, well before they felt any emotion for one another. Lyda was several years older than Shorty, and had never been in a long-term relationship with a man. Some had been serious, even intense, but they never lasted. The two recounted their life experiences; the pleasures they had loved, the sorrows they had endured.

Lyda's past became an open book; no secret withheld; no sin unconfessed. Shorty's past was judicially filtered through a lens of quiet recrimination. He revealed some secrets, and confessed the normal and usual sins. He told her about Shirley and the Preachers School, but could not admit his anger about the past. He dared not express his desire to avenge; his lust to get even.

Within a year, they married. Lyda was barren. No children would be born of their union, but Shorty knew that before the ceremony. It did not matter to him. What truly mattered was that he could believe Lyda, trust what she said and what she did. Lyda was not a woman to flaunt herself or flirt with customers. To Shorty, she emitted a warm glow of stability. She was a firm but gentle helpmate as he continued to wrestle with the guilt still lurking deep within his soul. Had he sinned that egregiously? Would his latent desire to preach ever be fulfilled? He knew God had forgiven him, but would others be so forgiving as Lyda?

Many customers walked into the grocery and selected the items they wanted. Others called in their grocery list to Lyda. She and her brother Tom would fill the order and deliver directly to the customer's home. The only problem with home deliveries was that there would be no immediate payment. Generally, the husband was at work and the wife didn't have the cash to pay. "Try to get you paid on Friday" became a familiar refrain. Lyda was always skeptical. Shorty always understood.

Shorty seldom made deliveries himself. Tom stocked the shelves, filled the orders and made deliveries. Lyda took care of the customers who walked into the store. Lyda never got out. She couldn't drive, and was very shy, or so it seemed. People said she was ashamed. Ashamed of being Shorty's wife. Ashamed of being an old maid, ready to marry the first man who looked her way, even if he was a cripple. But she wasn't ashamed of anything. She simply couldn't drive.

7.

A Witness – 1944

Not too far away from the grocery store, the First Fellowship Baptist Church was changing locations. The congregation consisted of families primarily from Kentucky, some of whom he knew from the customer base at the store. Shorty's brothers were attending, and they were inviting Shorty to visit. Marvin was the oldest brother, and physically quite different. Marvin was neither tall nor short, but he was robust, round and jolly. If he were in a sleigh, you'd think he was Santa Claus. Wilbur was the second-oldest brother. He was serious and grim-faced; he seldom smiled or laughed. Sometimes he would chuckle while holding his breath, never making a sound. But you knew Wilbur liked you if he gave you a wink of the eye.

"Got to hear this man preach, Shorty," Marvin and Wilbur would say. "He looks like that picture of Moses in your Bible – long, white hair, tall with broad shoulders and a voice that booms like a cannon. Believe if he ever shouted, he'd blow out the windows."

"Where is this new church, Wilbur?" Shorty asked. "How far away is it?"

"Go across the river, down Main Street and then you got to turn onto East Avenue. Go over the tracks a few blocks and look for a side street. I believe it's on Eleventh Street," said Walter.

"That's it," said Marvin, "Eleventh Street Baptist Church. They changed their name, and are meeting now in that old abandoned dance hall, you know, the one the city shut down a few months ago, maybe longer because of that murder. The muggings and whores didn't help either. Yeah, can you believe it? They've started a church in that old dance hall."

Shorty was familiar with the dance hall. He knew exactly where it was. He had been a visitor of sorts one Saturday night, not that long ago. A visit he longed to forget; a visit he wished he had never made.

But on that night, months earlier, Shorty had been restless. He had lain down to sleep, but never took off his clothes. It was Saturday night, and the moon had been full. He decided to go for a walk. He had draped his shoulders with a dark-blue summer jacket, and left his apartment. Meandering down B Street to the bridge, he headed east. He had kept walking, the ruffle of his footsteps the only sound rasping on the concrete sidewalk. He passed the Courthouse on Main Street, the storefronts and office buildings, all closed and dark, without interior lights. He kept walking, walking away from his apartment, moving at a steady pace with no particular destination as his goal. His mind wandered back to high school, to his age of innocence and naiveté. There was a time when he could have walked away, but he didn't. He couldn't determine if his feelings of guilt were driven by a sin he did commit, or by the sins he wanted to.

As he crossed the railroad tracks, he realized that he was on East Avenue, farther away from his apartment than ever before. But he continued to walk. He was now headed toward the East Side Dance Hall. Just two more blocks to Eleventh Street. He had heard about this place. He knew what lay ahead. He also knew that he should turn back. It was almost midnight. He had never stayed out this late before, and certainly not this far from home.

Then, he heard music, then laughter and shouts of glee. Before he could muster the moral courage to change his direction, he found himself standing next to a large tree. The tree had low limbs, with abundant foliage, and it stood in the front yard of an old house. Both the tree and the house guarded an alley that headed due north. The alley separated the small house from the dance hall. Aided by a single light over the front door, he could see the front porch of the dance hall. By the light of the moon, he could see across the porch to a vacant lot at the far side of the dance hall. Hidden in the tree's foliage, Shorty could not see his own shadow. But his view of the dance hall was clear and unimpeded.

As the front door to the dance hall opened, a man slowly exited. The music inside blasted out into the street. The man gently closed the door and leaned against the frame. He reached into his pocket for a cigarette. He was sweating profusely, and he had raised his hand to wipe his brow. He must have been dancing very hard. Out of the darkness of the vacant lot, another man suddenly appeared. At first, Shorty thought the second man was offering to light the man's cigarette, but then he saw the glove on his hand. It wasn't a match or a lighter that the second man had pulled from his pocket. It was a knife. And he was wearing an odd-looking pair of eyeglasses.

Shorty had taken a half step back, hiding himself behind the tree trunk. He had sneaked a peek around the tree trunk in silent horror, as the second man sliced the sweating man's throat. The wounded man grasped at his neck and slumped against the door frame. The assailant proceeded to stab the knife into his stomach, rotating the blade with ever-increasing pressure. Then the assailant spat, forcibly and with vengeance.

After the wounded man had collapsed on the front porch, the knife-wielding assailant took a step toward him and spat again. He gruffly mumbled words inaudible to Shorty. Then he viciously kicked the wounded man in the ribs while spitting for a third time, this time in the fallen man's face. The assailant walked carefully back to the edge of the porch and jumped onto the sidewalk. He walked casually into the vacant lot, and disappeared.

Shorty had been in shock. He had absentmindedly wandered into strange, perhaps forbidden territory, intending to leer at women dancing while men made fools of themselves. Instead, he had witnessed a murder.

As to the identity of the victim, he had no clue. But there was something eerily familiar about the assailant. Was it in the way he stood over the victim? The way he walked? Or was it the spitting?

In Shorty's youth, spitting had been a peculiar badge of honor among young boys pretending to be men. The better, further and more forcefully one could project saliva, the bigger, meaner and more feared you could be. It was an art form to be developed and perfected by a young ruffian on his way to becoming a full-grown thug. This assailant had become a master of the craft.

Shorty had seen a similar scene before. It was Shirley's old boyfriend spitting at her feet. She had cried. He had laughed and walked away. Shorty had been a silent, restrained and invisible witness to that scene, too. But that night on Eleventh Street, a myriad of thoughts and questions had raced through his mind. Should he stay or should he go? Should he knock on a neighbor's door and call the police? Should he attempt to aid the victim?

Then the front door to the dance hall opened. A blood-curdling scream filled the air. Shorty panicked. He slipped away into the darkness and secreted his way back to East Avenue, then to B Street, as fast as he could. He walked quickly, never looking back, as he scurried home to his apartment.

He had no business being out so late, and certainly no good reason to be at a dance hall. He had hoped the victim would survive the brutal attack, but Shorty had read the newspaper accounts. The victim had died; the assailant was still at large. Shorty had comforted himself believing he had no information that could aid in apprehending the assailant. Just as before, it would be best to restrain his instincts. To remain invisible; to maintain silence. The police would only ask questions he could not answer.

Except that there were some questions he would prefer not to answer. If asked, he would have had to answer, "Yes," he did have welder gloves. And, "Yes," he would have had to answer again, he did make knives. If the man's odd-looking glasses were actually welder's goggles, Shorty would have had to answer a third question in the affirmative. But he knew that silence would be his shield – and silent he resolved to be.

He mentally berated himself as he headed home. Why hadn't he stayed in his apartment? If he had been so restless, why didn't he just lie in bed and read? He loved to read. Had he been so lonely that he would seek out strangers for company?

During his walk home, Shorty resolved to never wander alone on the dark streets of Hamilton. If he ever ventured out again, it would be to a wholesome place.

If Marvin and Wilbur were right, he knew exactly where that place might be.

8.

Enduring Temptation – 1945

Shorty had been looking for a church to attend, searching for people he could talk to, sharing his enthusiasm for the Bible and all it meant to him. Eleventh Street Baptist could be a good place to visit, even though it was not within easy walking distance. Shorty had actual knowledge of how far the walk could be.

He had a reliable car and a grocery delivery van. He could drive to church and Tom could still deliver the groceries. Lyda didn't care much for church. Based upon what Shorty had told her, she was convinced that most churchgoing people were hypocrites. She also feared that more people than Marvin and Wilbur knew about Shorty's past indiscretions. Tom knew. Most of Corbin knew, or should have known. And it seemed as though all of Kentucky was relocating to Hamilton. There was bound to be someone who knew about, or at least had heard rumors of Shorty's sordid past. She felt as though people would judge her for something she didn't do. She didn't break up Shorty's marriage. Shorty just walked away from it all. Never really said why the marriage busted, just that it did. "That woman" was the way he always referred to her. And well, she was probably still in Kentucky, and would probably die there for all that Lyda knew.

One Saturday, Lyda got a call for groceries. Lady said she was new to town, but her family knew Shorty's family. They went to church with Marvin and Wilbur. Small talk and gossip later, Lyda was pretty sure the lady was telling the truth, so she took her order over the phone. Told her it would be early next week before delivery could be made. The store was out of flour and beans, but expecting delivery any time now to restock the shelves.

But that was not the total truth. Lyda wanted to check on the lady's story. She wanted to talk to Marvin to see if this woman was in the church with him and Wilbur. Even more importantly, would she pay the bill? Shorty never checked on anyone's credit. How could he? No credit cards, and only well-to-do people had a checking account. If you didn't have a job, you didn't have money. Where did her husband work?

Shorty decided to visit Eleventh Street Baptist that same Saturday night. The church convened on Saturday evenings, hoping to keep the older children of their congregation out of the pool hall and bars. They met again on Sunday morning and Sunday night. Wednesday prayer services were infrequent. Most of the members worked long hours during the week, and their children had school the next day. The preacher also worked long hours at his secular job and found it difficult to prepare a midweek sermon.

Saturday nights were more informal. Men often wore work clothes and children came in play clothes.

Some women, intent on looking their best for the Sunday morning service, had their hair in rollers covered with a hairnet. The crowd was of good size and there were two rows of pews as you faced the pulpit and the altar. Down from each side of the pulpit was a smaller pew, placed parallel and next to the outer wall. From the pulpit, you could see a small pew to your left, where some of the deacons sat. A small pew to the right was where visiting preachers or some young man who had just been called to preach would sit. Straight ahead, there were two rows of pews with an average-width aisle between them. This was the aisle you had to walk if you wanted to join Eleventh Street Baptist. Walk the aisle, confess your sins and ask Jesus to forgive you. The Baptist way. A public profession of faith.

Shorty felt drawn to sit near the pulpit. He wanted to hear what this preacher had to say. Wilbur said he looked like Moses and had the voice of a mighty wind. When he spread his arms, you just knew a sea or something was going to part. He was a force; he seemingly had the power of God. But he dared not to sit on a side pew. He was not a deacon, and sure enough, he wasn't a preacher. He knew he could preach, but just because you could would be no reason to put yourself up there in a pulpit and tell others how to live. Shorty didn't believe that he had any right telling people they were sinners. It would be like the pot calling the kettle black.

Shorty had surely sinned enough himself. He could tell you a thing or two about sinning. Even if he hadn't done it, he'd read about it. Yes, Shorty could tell you a lot about sinning, and how God didn't like those sort of things. But inside his heart, Shorty knew a lot about forgiveness too. And he knew that God forgave a lot. You only had to ask.

Shorty stayed away from the side pews and walked slowly down the aisle. Wilbur motioned to join him. Three rows from the front; good view; able to hear with no problem.

"Shorty, do you remember Ben? Yes, Ben Langley from back home? He's living here now and his son. Have you ever met his son, Ron? Here is Ron now, and his wife, Gail."

"Gail, Ron, this is Shorty, my brother."

Shorty looked at Gail directly in her eyes. He dared not look at other features she prominently displayed. She was a beautiful woman, dressed in a silk dress that was almost transparent. She raised her hand slightly, exposing long, slender fingers decorated with a huge diamond ring.

"What do you do for a living Ron, Shorty asked?"

"I deliver milk and eggs for the local dairyman's association. It's not the most prestigious job in the world, but it's steady work and the pay is always on time."

"And Gail? Are you a housewife?" asked Shorty.

"Oh yes, I just tend the house and look after Ron. He's Ben's only child, you know; been spoiled all his life. Expects me to do the same. Spoiling, yes, spoiling's what I do most of the time."

"Where do you shop for foodstuffs and groceries?" Shorty asked.

"Well, your brother said I should call your little store since you deliver and I haven't got a car. In fact, I placed an order with some woman at your store just this morning."

This morning? So Gail was the woman Lyda was asking about. Lyda had said to Shorty, "This woman sounds too young to be a housewife; doesn't even know you need flour to bake a cake; bet she can't cook worth a lick; how would you like to have a woman who couldn't cook? That would be a fine thing now, wouldn't it, Shorty?"

This morning, yes. Shorty remembered what Lyda had said. But from the looks of things, Shorty bet that Ron really didn't care if Gail could cook or not. Her job was to spoil him. She looked fully equipped to do just that.

After the service, Shorty realized that Eleventh Street Baptist could be a place to go for wholesome fellowship. He had certainly heard the gospel preached. Inwardly, the call for him to preach grew ever stronger. But Shorty didn't know for sure if the desire he felt was being spawned by a pure heart. He also felt shame. Was it pride that called him to envision himself in the pulpit, preaching and gazing into the congregation?

Would they admire his demeanor? Appreciate his preparedness? Would they understand his message? All those things could be developed and perfected with time. But would he be praised for his performance? Would his brothers encourage and support this decision? Would Lyda come to hear him preach? Could he still the lust of his flesh and restrain his wandering eye? Could he deflate the pride of his fragile ego? But most importantly, could he ever quiet the demons still lurking inside? The demons that still pushed him block by block to places he knew he should never go?

III.

"Behold, I stand at the door and knock: if any man hear my voice, and open the door, I will come in to him, and will sup with him, and he with me."

(Revelation 3:20).

9.

Saturday Night – Fall, 1945

Lucas arrived in Hamilton in the fall of 1945. His skin was yellow from the remnants of malaria. His feet were still raw with jungle rot. He had lost weight from a robust and fit one hundred and sixty pounds at enlistment to one hundred and fifteen upon discharge. He no longer carried a rifle. He carried a grudge.

It was Saturday night and Lucas still had money left from payday. His last payday at the plant. Dancing and drinking were on his mind. A long and liquid weekend lay in store. The dance hall on Eleventh Street had a reputation for fun, pretty girls and good times. That is where he would go tonight. The war was over, but the fight had not left Lucas. Dancing and drinking were just an excuse to set the stage for a fight. Few people carried a gun or knife. To fight with weapons was a cowardly act. Only criminals would try to permanently hurt or kill you. A good fight was an honorable event. Fisticuffs, wrestling, biting and hair pulling; these were the weapons of an honest fight. Lucas had fists of iron and biceps pumped like small cannonballs. At five foot six, he wasn't tall. But he was quick, agile and trained in martial arts. He had met the Japanese face to face during the war. He hadn't backed down, and he was still alive.

He recalled Pearl Harbor when he and his brother Julian were eating breakfast at Schofield Barracks. It was a Sunday morning. On the day that President Roosevelt said "would live in infamy," the Japanese Imperial Airforce attacked. Just out of basic training, and with no combat experience, Lucas and his fellow soldiers faced the first real fight of their life, and with no weapon within reach. They scurried from the mess hall, shouting and looking for their superior officer or anyone in charge. No one could be found. They ran to the munitions storage bins. They tore down the doors and ammunition cages with their bare hands. Grabbing rifles, pistols, machine guns and as much ammunition as they could carry, they climbed to the roof of Schofield Barracks.

A lowly private with no formal training, Lucas nevertheless took charge. He shouted instructions and encouragement. He carried two machine guns. He wrapped his neck and arms with as many rounds of machine gun ammo as he could carry. He was going to kill some Japs, and kill as many as he could. Hell, they'd just gone and made him mad.

But the war was over. Lucas wasn't mad enough to kill, just to fight. Lucas didn't back down from a fight. Almost always, after a good one, he'd realize that the whole episode was foolish, stupid and even dangerous. It was only a matter of time before some drunk pulled a gun and shot him. Martial arts, speed and agility would not be much help then for sure. But just as drinking was an excuse for fighting, fighting had also become an excuse. His whole lifestyle had become an excuse to avoid what he needed most. He knew what it was, but he was too proud to admit it. A small, sweet voice still haunted him. It was the voice of Maggie. "Lucas, are you saved?"

A dance hall's retreat from reality was nearly as bad as reality itself. One reality facing Lucas was that he needed a different job. In the plant, heavy cranes lifted, carried and moved rolls of steel from a storage area to a workstation where laborers guided the roll of steel carefully to the extended arm of a slitter machine. The roll of steel, with the strength of the crane and the guiding hands of the workmen, would slip onto the arm of the slitter, ready for the next phase of fabrication.

Each roll of steel weighed several tons, and it would be bound together by several small, thin metal braces. The binding was designed to prevent the coiled steel from breaking loose and unwinding in a wild, furious and dangerous wave.

The crane operator took great care to move slowly and align the roll of coiled steel to the arm of the slitter machine. If the roll of steel slid from the crane, or was bumped or tossed, the metal braces could break. When that happened, the coiled tension would release and let the power of eight-gauge steel flap and flop with tremendous force and fury.

Not only was it dangerous and a near-death experience for anyone standing close to the unloosed coil of steel, it was loud. The sound of the steel hitting the concrete floor; the shouts of those nearby and the cries of distant onlookers reminded Lucas of the planes dropping their bombs at Pearl Harbor. Work at the plant became a daily reenactment of the fight and the fear he'd felt, not only on that infamous Sunday, but during the battles he'd fought during the years that followed.

Some of his coworkers would laugh when Lucas dived under a bench or crawled to a corner, desperately reaching for a wrench or a hammer or anything he could use as a weapon to defend himself from attack. The war was over in Washington, but not for Lucas. He had fought like a crazed animal on the beaches and in the brush and jungles of the Pacific Islands. His infantry troop had spent more days in combat than any other unit in the war. Yet he was still fighting. Fighting like a caged animal in an industrial zoo. He couldn't take it anymore. Last Friday had been his final paycheck. But it was Saturday night now, and the East Side Dance Hall had been highly recommended. He might as well give it a try.

Lucas approached the porch and strolled up the steps. He stopped to touch, then lean on, the front door. The door was firm; no movement or sway. It was made of solid oak, strong and thick. Obviously designed to smother the noise and music of a dance hall, the East Side Dance Hall. He briefly considered how the door was mounted, brass-coated hinges holding the door to the frame, the lock and handle. He could not hear a sound. As he slowly opened the door, no music floated out, no loud singing or talking, no audible evidence of a party in progress. Then, he recognized a voice.

"Do you know the Lord today? Have your sins been forgiven? Are you tired and heavy laden? Do you need a Savior? Do you need to rest from your labor? Then why not come to Him tonight? Why not tonight?"

It was Pastor. Lucas would recognize that voice anywhere. What was Pastor doing in a dance hall? Was this a dance hall or something else? A church? How in the world did Pastor convert this place into a church? These and many more questions popped into Lucas's mind as he stood by the front door, halfway in, halfway out. Lucas also recognized the words.

These were the words of an altar call. Pastor had made this same plea more times than he could ever count. Pastor scanned the congregation, looking for a response, movement of any kind that would indicate that his sermon had taken hold. He was searching for evidence of the Holy Spirit at work. It appeared that every head was bowed and that no one was moving at all, yet Pastor felt a stirring in his own soul as he stepped to the side of the pulpit.

Pastor looked beyond the adults sitting in the front pews to the younger adults and teenagers nestled in the back of the sanctuary. He lengthened his gaze until he saw the front door, slightly ajar.

Pastor saw a young man standing with one foot and leg inside the threshold of the front door. The man was peering around the door with his shoulders exposed, peeking inside. The young man was better dressed than the people in the pews. He wore a suit, had at least one clean shoe, and was holding a hat in his left hand. He was leaning in and holding the door slightly open, almost closed. He looked confused. He looked as though he had stumbled into the building by mistake. Was this young man looking for someone, or did he have the wrong address? He also looked familiar.

"Softly and gently the Savior is calling, calling for you and for me."

Lucas knew these words by heart. He had heard them many times in his youth, standing outside of a church or looking for girls at campground revivals. But the words carried a different melody this night. Even though he had come to Eleventh Street to dance, he continued to stare toward the altar. He stepped all the way inside. He had recognized the voice. He understood the question. Now, he recognized the man.

He could not walk away from the front door. He crouched, squatting and resting on both knees just the way he did in the Army. Squatting to rest, to eat or drink, or to take a break at the first sound of "At Ease," but still alert and ready to burst into action. It seemed as though the Pastor's blue eyes were burning through his soul. Pastor's huge arms were extended, and inviting Lucas to come inside. To come inside and rest. To lay down a heavy burden, a burden he had been carrying for a long time.

But this was Saturday night and he was dressed in his best. Going to church was not his idea of a good time. Obviously, he had made a mistake. No one had told him that the dance hall had been shut down by the city. No one had told him that Pastor had relocated his church in that building. And who were the people inside? Some of the faces looked strangely familiar. But not tonight. Oh my, not tonight.

Lucas scoured the want ads looking for a job. He traveled around town, looking for projects under construction. He asked friends, neighbors and family if they knew of any work available. The job had to be outdoors. He was finished with indoor warfare.

Just outside of Cincinnati, a nuclear plant was under construction, with foundations and walls the depth and thickness of which Lucas had never seen. He was sure he could do any of the work that the project needed. He had learned how to build in the Army. It appeared they needed help, and he was willing to work, yet no immediate openings were available.

The vast majority of the men hired to build the plant would not begin work for another two, perhaps three weeks. The foundation and grading work had to be completed first. However, when the workers did arrive, the foreman expressed concern about hygiene and human waste. Would Lucas be willing to build an outdoor toilet for the job site? The foreman had two experienced carpenters to take the lead, but they needed a helper. Lucas readily agreed. He would help build the toilet. It was his first job outdoors since the war. He was building an outhouse.

The fresh breeze gently blew, with a clear sky and the warm sun on his face. It felt good. He thought about that Saturday night. He had thought it was a dance hall, but it was a church. He had intended to dance and drink, but he quietly considered a change to his way of life. Maybe it was time to settle down. Saturday night fights were not really fun. They were dangerous. Lucas actually despised fighting. He had fought long enough. It was his temper. His temper always seemed to get the best of him.

It was also embarrassing. He didn't want a fighter's reputation. A reputation for being a hothead; for being a quick-tempered jerk. When he didn't drink, he wasn't a hothead. Most of the time he was a patient person. He had proved that a hundred times over during the war.

He was not in the best of health, but he would get better. He knew that for sure. He always had. He would recover from the lingering effects of malaria; his feet would heal. He could also clear his mind by quitting the evil drink. He remembered his mother crying when his father came home drunk. It wasn't a pretty sight. Was he himself that disgusting when he was drunk?

Lucas wanted more than just survival. He wanted to live. To be more than being a builder of outhouses. He wanted to build a life. A life like Pastor had talked about back home; a life that Pastor had no doubt preached about that Saturday night. A life that he had often dreamed about with Maggie.

Maybe, just maybe, he could learn to do something worthwhile with his life besides drinking and fighting. He desperately wanted to escape the fears and nightmares of war – a war that had brought death to so many, so unexpectedly. He had hoped drinking would be an avenue of escape, but it had proved to be a detour to misery.

Lucas survived the war only by the grace of God. Deep down inside, he knew that. His sisters and friends back home said that they had prayed for his safety. He believed them. The power of prayer was something he had never possessed, but he had seemingly been its beneficiary. The prayers of God's chosen were a powerful tool. Pastor once said that the prayer of a righteous man availeth much. Lucas believed that too. A better life could be found. Perhaps even a peace could be made with the enemy – all of them.

10.

Finding A Good Thing – 1946 to 1950

Maggie Gibbs refused to visit Hamilton. Even though she had three sisters move north, Maggie was the youngest and still felt needed at home. Her mother was now a widow, and the sisters still in Kentucky had their own husbands and children to look after. Her brothers were in Indiana working construction, or running a gambling house. They were no help to the family. She would not go to Ohio as a favor to anyone other than herself. She would not visit, let alone consider moving from her home, without the prospects of a godly man in her life. Too many bars and honky-tonks in Hamilton. The eligible men? Well, she had heard far too many stories of degenerate behavior. Without a real reason to visit or to move, and without a reasonable prospect for a husband, she would stay with her mother, help on the farm and teach school.

She had taught school during the war. Grades one through eight were all in the same classroom. As confusing as it might first appear, it was an orderly system. The older children helped the younger and the younger inspired the older. Discipline was seldom at issue, because brothers and sisters would control their siblings and neighbors would tell on you. No one wanted to be disciplined at school, because it was only the precursor to a beating at home, or worse, the parents' refusal to send you back. That meant hard work at the farm, or in the quarry, or other manual labor that no one wanted to do.

All Maggie had to do was raise her hand about halfway, and point or wag her finger, and peace was immediately restored. She enjoyed being in charge. Being the baby of fourteen children had reinforced her sense of importance. She exerted the force of her will upon others. What Maggie wanted, she generally got. And in truth, she didn't want riches or fame. She just wanted a husband. A godly husband.

Too many of her childhood boyfriends had been killed or maimed in the war. She had written letters, dozens of letters, to those serving in the armed forces. She wrote about home, the weather, politics, church and friends. A few wrote back; many never replied; some never came home alive. She also wrote to Lucas. Those who did return with a sound body were often infected with a distorted mind. Those who managed to truly survive in mind and body sought greener pastures. They moved, following the jobs, and leaving the backbreaking work of a Kentucky farm behind. It would take years before life at home returned to normal, and Maggie didn't have years to wait.

Maggie knew Lucas was in Hamilton, and Lucas knew Maggie was still in London. Sisters on both sides kept them informed. The sisters also baited the hook, letting both Maggie and Lucas know of each other's singleness and availability. No suitable mate in the picture; no serious "sparking" going on. "Sparking" was a term Maggie's mother used when a boy expressed interest in one of her girls.

Maggie did not have to wait years. Lucas sought her out. He rode a train to London. He "sparked" and courted for nearly a week. He promised to live a better life, to be a good husband, to forsake the evil of drink. He even promised to attend church. He got down on one knee. He was serious. So was Maggie. He proposed marriage, but she did not accept, at least not right away.

The last time she and Lucas had heard a preacher together was in high school, shortly before the war. To her knowledge, Lucas had not darkened the door of a church since. Anybody could promise to do better, to quit certain things and even to attend church. But how long could they keep such promises? How much time would pass before the penitent pleader backslid into sin and degradation? Maggie wondered if the broomstick episode still had a lingering and duping effect on Lucas.

Did he really mean what he was saying? Only time could tell, she thought, and one week of good conduct and romantic promises was not long enough. Lucas would have to prove himself worthy of her hand in marriage. She would not let her emotions, or his handsome face, distract her from her marital vision. She wanted a husband, but not just any man would do. He must be a godly man. Certainly, a handsome man would be an added bonus.

Maggie mused to herself. This was going to be fun. Lucas, the valiant and brave soldier, humbled by a country girl. It was a wonderful feeling; a sight to behold. She couldn't wait to accept his proposal.

Under the supervision of Lucas's sister Sadie, Maggie visited Hamilton. Lucas was on his best behavior and escorted Maggie to Eleventh Street Baptist, with Hank and Sadie as chaperones. They spent Saturday night under the preaching of Pastor, and Sunday morning as well. On Sunday afternoon, Maggie took the train back to London, Kentucky, where she was greeted by her mother with an inquisitive smile. Had she accepted? Had she said "yes" to the young man Mother Gibbs so thoroughly admired? "Not just yet," Maggie replied. "I so love the train ride. It gives me time to think."

Her monthly visits by train soon accelerated to weekly trips from London to Hamilton. On her last trip, she was offered employment as a secretary to a bank officer. Maggie could type over sixty words per minute on the bank's new Underwood manual typewriter, with few or no errors. With her background as a schoolteacher, she learned the basics of banking, loan applications and bookkeeping. With a job, a safe apartment and a cadre of new friends at church, Maggie was ready to be Lucas's wife. Lucas had been true to his word. Maggie would accept. Her mother and sisters would be overjoyed. They had learned to love Lucas, too.

It was a simple wedding. Maggie's mother and one sister attended and served as witnesses. Lucas gave the preacher ten dollars and a hearty handshake. He kissed

Maggie for the very first time. He enjoyed it. So did Maggie.

He borrowed a car from Delmer, one of Maggie's old "boyfriends," in exchange for a promise to return it with a full tank of gas. They honeymooned at Cumberland Falls, near Somerset. As promised, Lucas returned the car, but offered Delmer three hundred dollars for the certificate of title. Delmer hesitated, hoping Lucas would take the train back to Hamilton as he had so many times before. Delmer, who had a deformed hand and did not serve in the Army, had primped and pined for Maggie all through the war years. When Delmer realized that Maggie and Lucas were married, he accepted the offer. Delmer may have lost Maggie, but he gained three hundred dollars for a worn-out Ford. He was happy. Lucas was ecstatic.

Church membership continued to grow at Eleventh Street Baptist. The congregation ranged in age from infants in arms to great-grandparents. There were many families with children, as well as singles of all ages. Widows grieved the loss of their husbands; single women were still looking for a mate. For many of them, the prospects of marriage were growing dimmer every day.

In the congregation this morning were some first-time visitors. They were surprised at how many people they knew. Many of those in attendance were either from Kentucky or had relatives still living there. In so many ways, visiting Eleventh Street Baptist was like a homecoming, with familiar faces and similar backgrounds – everyone from humble beginnings, and each looking for a fresh start. Several sweet families with precious children occupied the pews, and yes, men too. Young, strong, single men, with jobs.

It was after eleven o'clock in the morning and Pastor had yet to preach. Two young men on the side pew had asked Pastor for a chance to speak. Just a few minutes to say a few words. The first young man spoke for nearly forty-five minutes. "Just a few words," he'd said, "just to thank Jesus for saving my soul and calling me to preach." And indeed, he was thankful. You could tell he was thankful. He said so repeatedly. Based upon what he said he had done in his life, he should have been thankful that the good Lord hadn't struck him dead or turned him into a pillar of salt.

The congregation had come to hear Pastor preach. He looked exactly like what they had heard about him. He was tall, with strong, broad shoulders. His white hair was cut long and curled over his ears. If a movie about Moses should ever be made, Pastor could play the role. He was an impressive sight to behold. But it was his voice that everyone admired and talked about. "His voice is so strong," they'd say. "You can hear him as far as East Avenue on a summer's day with the windows open."

East Avenue was several blocks away from Eleventh Street. It needed to hear the gospel as much as those in the pew this morning. Half of the bars in Hamilton were on East Avenue, and many were opening up again on Sunday morning after a Saturday night of sinful recreation. Drinking, gambling and whoring; East Avenue had it all. But it was within earshot of Pastor, and Pastor would soon be preaching if only the second young man called to preach could ever stop crying.

Pastor had been gracious to the first young man, and had thanked him for being so thankful. The second young man said that he too had been called to preach. But he was so overcome with joy that he couldn't speak. He cried. He just cried, and continued crying for nearly fifteen minutes, until Pastor placed his strong hands upon his shoulder and gently half-hugged and half-tugged him back to his seat.

Pastor was next, and everyone said he would be worth the wait. "Don't worry about the time," they would insist. "It may be twelve noon or later, but just wait until he gets started. The pirit of the Lord is going to fill the house today."

Shorty was speechless. The power that ran through this man was difficult to understand, and impossible to describe. Pastor's voice brought men to tears and women to their knees. The children, even babies, fell silent. It was as though a spell of sanctification had been sprinkled upon everyone in the building. Rough, callused men humbled themselves. Their wives shouted with joy because the Lord had saved their men from eternal damnation. "Oh, he is a good man. He works hard to support our family, but he was lost. But praise be to God, now he is found."

Young children tearfully walked the aisle. Some came running, others sprinted toward the altar. There was something going on today that Shorty had never witnessed before. The Lord was working – and Pastor, he was an instrument in God's mighty hand. And he wasn't even finished with his sermon.

Lucas had been standing in the doorway ever since the second young man began crying. He witnessed how Pastor led the young man gently to his seat, and with a dramatic and swift turn toward the congregation, began his sermon. He had seen the response to Pastor's message. He remembered that spring night in Kentucky, at the outdoor camp meeting, when Pastor had spoken about many of the same things. He remembered one question in particular. The question Maggie had asked.

Lucas had not completely closed the door. He had knelt to one knee, huddling low, holding the door slightly ajar, ready to escape, poised to flee and hoping to remain invisible. He was afraid to stay, but unable to leave.

He had not been faithful to church as he had promised Maggie. In three years of marriage, he had visited the church only three times. Three Easter services; three visits. But he and Maggie now had a child. Things were truly different. Everything was different but Lucas.

He was still working hard, seven days a week. There was no time for church. In the evenings he worked for Hank, trying to repay him for raising his younger sisters and baby brother.

Even while he worked, and especially at night, he tried to forget the deaths of his brothers in Europe. He tried to repress the memories of battle and the men he had killed, both intentionally and by mistake. And through it all, Maggie had not badgered Lucas to come to church. She never pouted or complained, but since the birth of their son, she had joined Eleventh Street Baptist and taken young Mark with her to every service. Mark was named after Lucas's slain brother. Marcus had been killed in World War II during the Battle of the Bulge.

Maggie sat four rows from the pulpit. With young Mark in her arms, barely a year old, she wondered why Pastor went silent. He was leaving the pulpit and slowly walking down the steps to the altar. When he stopped walking, he gradually raised his head and looked toward the ceiling as though searching for something or someone in the rafters. He appeared to be praying, mumbling phrases, perhaps verses of scripture. The words he uttered were not comprehensible. Was he speaking to someone? Someone with greater authority?

Pastor took a deep breath and turned his broad shoulders to the congregation. Then he faced down the aisle toward the front door. People in the congregation could tell that Pastor's eyes had focused on something behind them, back to the entrance of the church. A few tried to sneak a peek over their shoulder without appearing to do so. Others, more toward the rear of the building, could turn sideways and observe what Pastor saw. It was a well-dressed man, halfway down on his knees, crouching, almost hugging the door frame, and silently crying.

Pastor resumed talking, but the sound of his voice gradually lowered. Instead of preaching at his normal high octave, his tone became one of pensive pleading. He knew who stood at the door. He had prayed for this man. He had loved him since he was just a child.

Maggie turned to watch Pastor. He moved slowly but steadily past her. As she followed his footsteps, she saw the object of Pastor's attention. With a quick glance, she saw Lucas. He was on one knee at the front door, leaning into the frame, his head bowed and bobbing. It looked as if he was crying.

Maggie was afraid to turn completely around. She feared to face in his direction. Feared that their eyes would meet. She feared that Lucas would stand up and walk away. She had prayed for this moment. She had wept while changing Mark's diaper and putting him to bed. She had begged the Lord to intervene in their marriage, hoping that Lucas would one day truly repent.

Lucas had tried in his own strength to reform. Like the other women in the church who spoke of their husbands, Maggie could say that Lucas was a hard worker, a good man, a good husband. But both Maggie and Lucas knew he would turn out to be a father just like his own without divine intervention. Maggie turned to face the altar and began to pray, "O Lord, let this day be the day."

As Pastor walked the aisle toward the front entrance, Lucas slowly looked up. Their gaze locked. Pastor extended his strong right hand, and bent over to the penitent man before him. Lucas's whole body was trembling. Tears were running down his cheeks. Lucas took his hand and Pastor raised him to a standing position, gently hugging him, as Lucas laid his tear-stained cheek on Pastor's shoulder.

"Oh, God, forgive me," Lucas whispered. Pastor just sweetly smiled and whispered into Lucas's ear, "Though your sins be as scarlet, they shall be as white as snow."

Fred Lawrence began to hum, then quietly sing words to the hymn, "Lord, I'm Coming Home." As he continued, others joined in, the volume of their combined voices gradually rising until everyone had joined the chorus. "I've wandered far from away from God, but now I'm coming home. Coming home, coming home. Never more to roam."

With Pastor's hands draped over Lucas's shoulders, they walked back down the aisle together. Several people already stood at the altar, waiting to greet them. The pews began to empty as the entire congregation gathered to hug and embrace or lay a hand on him, his body still trembling as he continued to weep. He was greeted by all with tears of joy, rejoicing with him and with Maggie.

Lucas spoke softly, his voice broken with tears. He asked forgiveness from those around him, even though he had never harmed or caused shame to anyone present. He tearfully asked for their prayers and encouragement. He would try to be a better husband and father. He wanted more than anything to shelter his son from the trials he had endured, and the temptations he had faced.

Pastor continued to hug Lucas's shoulder as a line formed to shake his hand. The singing resumed, with Fred Lawrence leading the congregation in the song, "Victory in Jesus." After the last person to shake hands stepped aside, Maggie embraced Lucas at the altar. They hugged and cried onto each other's neck, alternately saying, "I love you" and I'm sorry," until a calm settled on them both. Lucas picked up Mark and held him chest high with his left arm, while he hugged Maggie with his right. He smiled. He had made it home at last. He had found a good thing.

"This is the day the Lord hath made," Pastor sounded in a loud voice. "Let us rejoice and be glad in it." And the whole church said, "Amen."

11.

The Next Step – Winter, 1950

Baptists baptize. That's what they do. That's how they got their name. Baptism for believers only. No infants, please. Baptism comes after you have confessed to the Lord Jesus Christ. Not required for salvation, but essential to an obedient believer. No sprinkling; no pouring; no holy water – but complete immersion, preferably in moving water. *Baptizein* is a Greek verb which means to immerse. The Greek word was never translated into English. King James of England had been sprinkled, and the men he hired to translate the Bible may well have feared for their life if they had translated the word as "immerse." So, it was "transliterated." Behold! A new word in the English vocabulary: "baptize." The Baptists were confident that immersion was the original method of baptism, and used well before the 1611 Edition of the Holy King James Bible. It was used by John the Baptist and the New Testament churches. If it was good enough for John the Baptist, it was good enough for Eleventh Street Baptist.

The Lutherans and Methodists, even the Presbyterians and Episcopalians might sprinkle or pour, but they were part of the Reformation. They had split and revolted from the authority of the Roman Catholic Church. They protested; they were the Reformers, they were Protestants. The Baptists did not need to be reformed; they had not protested anything. They were never part of the Roman Catholic Church. They refused to be called Protestants.

A good Baptist traced his heritage back to the time of Christ and the first church at Jerusalem, not to the early sixteenth century and Martin Luther. The Baptists may have been known by different names over time, but to a Baptist, it was evident that the Bible and impartial secular history sustained their claim to apostolic church succession. It was their ancestors who suffered as martyrs, and at the hands of the organized church at Rome.

But this view was not universally accepted. Even the Southern and Northern Baptist Associations abandoned this view of history. This difference in historical perspective was just one reason why Eleventh Street was so fiercely independent. They were not members of any formal convention, nor did they associate with other churches that were governed by or acquiesced to the authority of an organized hierarchy. Eleventh Street was a self-governed body, and the Bible was their only guide. The Bible was the inerrant word of God. If was good enough for Paul and Silas, it was good enough for them.

Lucas had more than changed his ways, he had truly repented. His mind and heart had been transformed. He had made a profession of faith before God and in the presence of witnesses. He was a believer in the truest sense of the word. Biblical baptism was his next act of obedience.

So, on the appointed Sunday, Lucas packed an older pair of slacks, a shirt and a change of socks into a brown paper bag. He took the bag with him as he, Maggie and young Mark headed to church. Pastor spoke about the two ordinances of the church, baptism and the Lord's Supper. Both sacraments were found in scripture; both were commanded to be observed by the faithful. He invited all to attend the baptismal ceremony to follow immediately after the church service.

The baptism would take place on the other side of town, next to the banks of the Little Miami River. Everyone knew the spot. It was just above the dam. He kept his sermon shorter than usual. It would take at least thirty minutes to get to the river's edge. Church was over by half-past twelve.

The congregation filed out of the building. Those who had cars invited those who did not to ride with them. Nearly twenty cars were filled by people desiring to witness Lucas's baptism. Pastor led the way in his pickup truck. Lucas fell in behind him, and the other cars jockeyed for position in the queue.

Eleventh Street did not have an indoor baptismal pool. Pastor often spoke of the benefits an indoor pool could offer, and had borrowed blueprints from a church that had constructed one in their facility. With an indoor pool, no one would have to travel after the service. Baptisms could be performed all year round, rain or shine, heat or cold. Pastor would push for a baptismal pool in the next building, even though a number of the church membership was against the idea.

Pastor argued that Paul and Silas probably used an indoor pool to baptize the Philippian jailer and his family. He argued and pleaded, but to no avail. The older members would righteously resist. Some would even leave to join another church. Paul and Silas couldn't trump Jesus. Jesus Himself was baptized outdoors, in the Jordan River no less. If a river was good enough for Jesus, it was good enough for them.

The procession eased onto East Avenue and headed north to Main Street. Not everyone made it through the first traffic signal. Those who did continued to follow Pastor as he turned left and headed west on Main Street. By the third traffic signal, the entire queue was headed west on Main Street toward the bridge over the Little Miami River. After crossing the bridge, Pastor turned right on B Street and headed north again. The river was on his right-hand side, flowing south toward the great Ohio River.

Pastor drove almost a mile up B Street. He passed several small businesses, all closed on Sunday. He passed the big paper plant to a wide grassy area by the road on his right. The paper plant often dumped dye into the river. Depending on the color of paper being made, the river could be either green, red or yellow. But today, the river was clear. The wide grassy area covered about an acre of open space, large enough for ten to fifteen cars to park. The ground sloped gently down to the riverbank. The remaining cars parked parallel with the road, slightly off the pavement. Some went further ahead, made a U-turn and parked on the other side of the road, facing back toward town.

The sky was clear, but it was cold, with the temperature in the high thirties. The river was flowing and crystal clear. There was no ice to shatter with an axe or hatchet, but Pastor had both in his truck just in case. The witnesses were bundled in heavy coats, and families huddled together, seeking each other's body heat. Pastor took off his suit coat and shoes; Lucas had already changed pants, and he too was barefoot.

They grasped each other by the arm and walked carefully down the slope to the river's edge. They looked at each other briefly, and gingerly stepped into the water. The water was cold, very cold, and moving swiftly at their feet. The river bottom was smooth, with a gradual slope. After a few more steps, Pastor and Lucas stood waist deep in the Little Miami River. Lucas shivered and rubbed his hands together. He blew his breath into his hands for warmth and turned to face Pastor. Pastor raised his right arm and nodded toward Fred Lawrence. It was time.

Fred began to sing, "Shall We Gather at the River." Everyone knew the words. They sang the song in harmony, braving the winter wind. Their voices echoed through the trees, and the wind carried their words downstream with the flow of the Little Miami.

"Yes we'll gather at the river," they continued. Those who had lost loved ones to the sting of death envisioned them with angels, all standing on a crystal shore by a river in heaven.

"The beautiful, the beautiful river," as they began the chorus. They longed to join a departed friend or family member. They imagined what it would be like to actually gather with the saints at the river that flows by the throne of God.

When they finished singing, Pastor raised his arm again. A still quiet descended. The only sounds came from wind rustling through nearby trees, and the river's steady current, cascading over small boulders.

Then Pastor spoke, "You are gathered here today to witness Brother Lucas follow our Lord's example and command. Baptism is a picture of Christ's death, His burial and His resurrection. It is a sacred ordinance of the church."

Pastor turned to face Lucas.

"Lucas, have you repented of your sins and asked God to forgive you?"

"I have," Lucas replied.

"Do you accept Jesus Christ as your Lord and Savior?"

"I do," said Lucas.

"Then, by the authority granted unto me, I do baptize you, my brother, in the name of the Father, and of the Son, and of the Holy Spirit."

Pastor held a handkerchief in his right hand and placed it over Lucas's mouth. With his left hand, he held the back of Lucas's neck and strained to lower him into the cold, running water of the river.

"Buried with Him by baptism into death," Pastor said while Lucas lay prone, almost floating and totally submerged;

"That like as Christ was raised up from the dead by the glory of the Father, even so we also should walk in newness of life," Pastor continued, as he struggled to lift Lucas back to his feet.

Pastor was not a young man anymore. His shoulders were racked stiff by arthritis. He ached. The cold water chilled him to the bone. His knees felt frozen. His feet and toes were numb. With the wet handkerchief still in his right hand, he wiped his brow, then his nose. The wind pulled tears from his eyes. He suddenly felt very weak.

Lucas was wet, head to toe. And cold. But he felt fine. His shirt and pants clung tightly to his flesh, nearly transparent. Despite the chilly breeze, Lucas felt a warmth inside his chest and throat. His eyes were clear; his spirit clean. Too long he had tried to make it on his own. Today was the day that would begin the rest of his life. Today, he was still a man, but a man saved by the grace of God. He had survived. He had survived the beaches and the bars. It was time to live, truly live. With his bare hands, he wiped the wetness from his face, and turned again to face Pastor.

They embraced, and Pastor began to lead Lucas back to shore. No more LVTs to exit. No more bullets to dodge. No more cries from wounded friends. Only shouts of "Amen" could Lucas hear. One woman hollered, "Praise be to God!" Others hooted, clapped their hands and stepped forward to greet the drenched and newly baptized saint. Everyone was moving. It was cold.

Fred Lawrence began another song. The crowd joined in vigorously to the hymn. "We're bound for the Promised Land." They continued to sing as they returned to their cars for the trip home. Sunday services were concluded. It had been a long day.

Maggie knew the words to that song as well. As Lucas half walked, half stumbled out of the water, their eyes met. Maggie silently mouthed the chorus, "Oh, who will come and go with me?"

Shivering in the cold, Lucas took her hand. They walked up the gentle slope to their car. Standing near the hood, Lucas eased out of his wet shirt and pulled the dry one out of the paper bag. He opened the car door and sat facing the river to change his socks. He decided not to change out of his wet pants. People still lingered in view, and Maggie begged him not to strip down in public. He walked around and over to the driver's side. Maggie dried the front seat where he had sat and joined him in the car. Mark lay asleep in the back seat. Maggie smiled and reached to touch his hand. They were finally bound for the Promised Land. Together.

12.

Easter Service

Pastor was correct. Easter Sunday had drawn a huge crowd. Folding chairs were positioned behind the back row of pews, and down each side of the center aisle. In corners and next to the side pews, wooden folding chairs borrowed from the funeral home sprinkled the auditorium. Small cardboard fans were placed in each folding chair and throughout each pew. The fans displayed the funeral home's name, address and brief advertisement of their services.

With no air conditioning, the temperature in the church rose steadily. The natural warmth of a beautiful spring morning made its contribution to the swelling heat. Pastor could sense a groundswell of emotion, slowly mounting with the heat, as the congregation began to enter and take their seats.

As the congregants entered the sanctuary, they greeted one another, shook hands and made small talk. Some quietly laughed while telling a short story, quickly regaining their composure. Today, they greeted each other more warmly, but with solemn sincerity on their faces. There was a recognizable glint of subdued joy in their eyes. Their demeanor exhibited an awareness that they were about to participate in something special. They had not come to socialize; they had come to worship. Today was Easter.

Beautifully stained rails wrapped themselves around the pulpit. The rails were waist high, the tops were rounded and beveled as wide as one's grip, smooth and firmly in place. This was the altar where so many had come to kneel, grip the rail and release a lifetime of pent-up strife and trials. The altar was a symbol of repentance, and Pastor had prayed that his sermon would draw many to their knees in front of it.

Several men served as ushers, guiding people to a seat. A visitor would sometimes take the seat of a member who had unofficially, but quite publicly claimed a certain pew as his own. In a normal service, the displaced member would awkwardly ask the visitor to move, but not today. The ushers directed all visitors to the uncontested seats, reserving the members' designated spots.

Teenage boys were assigned the task of opening the windows and holding the back and front doors open. Pastor and the deacons were silently praying for a gentle and cooling breeze to circulate through the sanctuary. As the time approached to begin the service, the low murmurings and whispers of the congregation grew more distinct. Some of the men began loosening their neckties or taking off their suit coats. Women held the funeral home fans and flickered them quickly, trying to entice a trace of moving air to their faces. The temperature was rising. It was going to be a hot morning in church.

Boys who normally wore blue jeans and a t-shirt to church were dressed in suits and sporting a clip-on necktie or bowtie. The younger girls were in their newest dresses to complement their freshly coiffed hair. Many wore a bow or ribbon, stylishly and strategically placed. All of the adult women wore a hat. Some of the hats were very functional and ordinary, but a few were outstanding, with peacock-like feathers, large brims, colorful and free flowing.

The women wore a hat to symbolize their submission to the Lord and to their husband. No one could find the biblical passage that required this act of submissive symbolism, but all remembered Pastor's sermon on the subject. They felt obliged to show respect, especially on Easter Sunday. Only the older women wore a hat to every church service, but Easter was also a good excuse to buy a new hat to match a new dress.

Most of the men looked uncomfortable in their formal attire. Few of the suits were new. Most of them were purchased years ago, or were received as hand-me-downs from a friend or family member of roughly the same size. Those who didn't wear a suit still strung a tie around their neck, draping down a worn and weary dress shirt. Working men had little time or money to shop for clothes. If clothes were truly needed, they bought a pair of sturdy pants or work boots. Fathers pinched their unruly children into silent obedience. Mothers stared down the teenagers who were paying too much attention to each other as the service began.

Easter Sunday service at Eleventh Street Baptist Church would be followed by communion, and a foot-washing service. No visitor would stay after church for either service. Only members were permitted to participate. It was a closed communion. Being saved, baptized and a member of a Baptist church was a good thing, but if you were not a member at Eleventh Street, and a member in good standing, you could not join in their communion service. The "closed communion" stance was another reason for their independence, and their refusal to be a part of a larger convention of churches.

Although all members in good standing were invited to stay and commune with their brothers and sisters in Christ, a majority of the membership would not. Family dinners, Easter egg hunts and other activities outside of church had been planned. Their schedule could not accommodate such an extended time at church. These and other reasons were sincerely given to justify their absence. Everyone knew the order of service: preaching, communion, foot washing. Only a few would dedicate their entire day to worship.

Sunday school for the children had concluded without incident or injury, and the service began promptly at eleven that morning. Fred Lawrence asked the Singleton family to help him lead the congregation in singing hymns. Brother Lawrence's voice had been growing steadily weaker over the years. A large congregation with the windows wide open had difficulty hearing him call out the page number. If they found the right page in the hymnal, they never knew when he had started to sing. He kind of mumbled his way into a song and waited to be drowned out.

The entire Singleton family was in attendance, and they could sing. Will and Bess Singleton, with their five sons, could sing bass through tenor, touching every note on the scale, in perfect harmony, and without accompaniment. Will Singleton stood up from his seat at the end of the small pew to the right of the pulpit. This was the deacon's pew, and Will had been a deacon of the church for many years. He placed his pack of Red Man chewing tobacco on the floor next to the empty Maxwell House coffee can that he used as a spittoon. He motioned for Bess and the boys to join him. They all walked to the front, and up two steps to the pulpit area. They turned and faced the congregation.

Will pulled the circular pitch pipe out of his shirt pocket. He blew into the pipe, one note at a time, blowing notes C, E and G. Bess and the boys hummed until they all were in harmony. Then off they took, singing at full strength. One of the sons had been in jail just hours before, bailed out by his oldest brother so that mother Bess would be in a singing mood. She hated it when one of her sons was in trouble with the law, and it seemed that one of them always was. But, according to Bess, they were good boys, just curious about life and such. They didn't mean any harm. "Boys will be boys," she always said.

She took comfort in Pastor's advice. "Train them up in the way they should go, and when they're older, they won't depart from it."

It was a good paraphrase of scripture, but many wondered if the youngest son would live long enough to reconsider and return to the way he was raised. That brought up another issue: Just how was he being raised?

He sang like an angel in church, but he hooted with the owls on Saturday night. When he sang "How Great Thou Art," it was the first time anyone at Eleventh Street had heard the song. It wasn't in the hymnal, but George Beverly Shea had sung it during a Billy Graham crusade. The youngest Singleton had seen the performance on television while drinking at a neighborhood saloon. Anyway, it appeared that their troubles made mother Bess's voice more mournful and powerful. The tears of a mother could move a crowd to real emotion.

After the congregation as a whole had finished singing, the Singletons huddled close together. They whispered to each other, confirming who would sing lead, bass, baritone, alto, soprano and tenor. The next song would be the finale, and the whole congregation knew what was next. It was an Easter tradition. It was the Singletons' favorite Easter song: "Up From the Grave He Arose."

With Will blowing into the pitch pipe once more, they fell into perfect harmony, singing *a cappella.* Tears flowed freely in the sanctuary. When the last "Amen" sounded, they walked back to their seats in complete silence. A holy hush had fallen over the congregation. No one stirred except Pastor. He slowly rose from his chair and approached the pulpit.

Aspiring young preachers had jammed themselves into the side pew to the left of the pulpit. Normally, only one or two young men would present themselves, seeking an invitation to speak. Today, there were four. It was obvious that they were cramped and uncomfortable sitting in the small pew. But Easter was worth the pain and suffering. If Pastor called upon one of them to speak on this special day, in front of such a huge gathering, a career as a minister of the gospel would get an immediate jump start. Perhaps they would be asked to substitute in a church while the full-time preacher was sick or on vacation. It could be the springboard to lead a revival service. If all went really well, they might be invited to preach at a church conference or to be a special guest. Easter Sunday could be a career maker. They were ready to preach.

As Pastor settled in behind the pulpit, he opened his Bible and said, "Will you please take your Bible and open to the Gospel of John, Chapter 13. Let us begin with a word of prayer."

None of the four "want-to-be" preachers would be invited to speak today. Their preparation had been for naught.

Lucas had never participated in a communion or a foot-washing service. He listened intently to Pastor's teaching. Intellectually, he understood why the ordinances were performed, and in a spiritual sense, why they were so special. But he was wary of the ordeal to come, and apprehensive about his role in it.

The communion service would be a somber and quiet event, with unleavened bread distributed among the members as they silently prayed and took a personal inventory of their life. Each member repented again for sins past, and for some relatively current. No wine would be served. There were too many veterans still struggling with the memories of war, and yearning for the temporary relief that alcohol offered. And it was too tempting for the younger believers. There was no sense giving them a taste of the forbidden fruit at such a tender age. And one of the Singleton boys had been in jail just last night on a charge of public intoxication. No, no real wine today, even if real wine was used by Jesus at the Last Supper. Grape juice would be the biblical substitute for communion. Welch's Grape Juice; several bottles on hand. Couldn't have an inebriated congregant disrupt the service.

Lucas was confident that he could maneuver through that service, but the foot washing to follow was weighing heavily on his mind and heart. "Whose feet will I wash," he asked himself, "and who will wash my feet?" As he pondered these questions, he reflected even more. "Who would even want to wash my feet?"

Four years in the Pacific Islands, and stomping through jungles drenched with a constant rain, had had an effect on Lucas. The effect was more than mental or emotional; the effect was physical as well. Upon his return from the war, he suffered from malaria, and for months he bore a yellow hue over his entire body. The symptoms of malaria would eventually disappear, but the jungle rot on his feet had not. Days and weeks of continually moving on foot while in wet socks and soaked military boots had infected the skin of his feet, and destroyed the contour and appearance of his toenails. Ingrown toenails and discoloration made his feet look grotesque. And they hurt. After a day on the job, having walked and sweated throughout the day, his feet would swell and even emit a foul odor. To take off his shoes and socks in church would be a source of extreme embarrassment. Who in the world would want to wash the feet of Lucas? Even Lucas did not relish the thought of washing his own feet.

When Pastor made the altar call, only a few came forward that Easter morning. Pastor viewed Easter service as a special time for believers. Though he wanted the lost sinner to be saved, his sermon was designed to encourage the faithful. He meant to reinforce their faith in a risen Savior – to remind them that they served a living Lord.

He also hoped that the members would silently prepare themselves for the communion service to follow, and that prayerful introspection would occur during his sermon, so that they would be spiritually cleansed and ready to eat the unleavened bread, a symbol of Christ's sinless body. And to drink, at least figuratively, his blood, as symbolized by the grape juice. The entire service was to be conducted in grateful admiration of Christ's sacrifice for their sins.

From a practical point of view, too many repenting sinners at the altar on Easter Sunday would delay the scheduled program of events. Easter would be a long day for the faithful. Jerry Sullivant prayed the benediction, and his prayer, though normally long, concluded very quickly.

Jerry Sullivant could really pray. His prayers could help you learn the Bible from Genesis to Revelation. Praising God for creation in the first chapter of Genesis, Jerry could lead you to Abraham and Isaac, to Moses crossing the Red Sea and the wilderness journey, through most of the prophets, his favorite New Testament references, all the way to the last chapter of Revelation. And he'd do it all while on both knees, with his hands raised toward heaven. It was an awesome thing to observe and to hear. When Jerry would finally beg and plead for Jesus to come again and to do so quickly, you knew he was almost finished. That was the same prayer of John the Revelator in the last chapter of the Bible.

But today, Jerry's prayer was simple and short. It was also sweet. He gave thanks that he served a risen Savior, and asked that God bless and protect every family represented in the service today. He prayed that everyone who was going home would travel safely, and that everyone who was staying would be blessed by what was to follow. Then, he simply said "Amen." The main service was over. All the people said "Amen," and the shuffle began to leave the pews and move toward the front door.

As the crowd exited the building, men began removing folding chairs and stacking them in a room behind the pulpit, preparing the sanctuary for the communion service to immediately follow. A table was placed before the altar, several feet away from the front pew. Women arranged the trays of unleavened bread for distribution and poured the grape juice into two large ornate cups, which they placed on the table. One cup was designated for the women, a separate cup for the men. God loved them all just the same, but for communion and foot washing, all the women would sit together on one side of the aisle, with all the men on the other side.

The church was nearly empty. The congregants now outside and in front of the church visited with each other. They complimented the children for their good behavior, and the women for looking so fine on a beautiful Sunday morning. A few men took the opportunity to smoke a cigarette and stretch their legs, knowing that the communion and foot washing service could take an hour or more. The length of the service would depend on how many members elected to go back inside to participate.

After twenty minutes, Wilbur appeared at the front door and dryly announced that it was time to begin the service. Lucas headed back to the front door, followed by Fred Meadows. They had been talking about a new job Fred had been offered. There might also be some work for Lucas this coming week.

Ben, his wife and Ron soon followed, but Gail feigned an upset stomach. She asked to be excused from the service. She said that she would go home by herself; that she would take the car. She told Ben that he could drive Ron to the house after the foot-washing service concluded. Ben wondered if Gail was truly not feeling well, or just didn't want to participate. In either event, it didn't matter, because Gail could be a distraction to the men in the service.

Everyone is supposed to be in prayerful mood, looking straight ahead or with their head bowed, but some of the men at Eleventh Street had excellent peripheral vision. In the last foot-washing service, Gail pretended to be completely innocent of her surroundings. Yet, she demurely exposed so much of her leg as she took off her hose that one man across the aisle, not as prayerful as he should have been, nearly fell out of the pew. It was just as well that she decided to absent herself from a ritual that deserved a pure mind and reverential spirit.

The communion service began with a prayer by Pastor. The person he wanted to lead the opening prayer was not seated in the sanctuary. Pastor looked toward Wilbur and Marvin with an inquisitive look. Their response, almost in unison, was a shrug of the shoulder, with an eyebrow slightly raised. Shorty had mentioned to Wilbur that Lyda was not feeling well and that he might have to go home to check on her. Lyda seldom came to church, but she seemed to support Shorty's desire to attend each service, and even to begin his own Wednesday night prayer and Bible study sessions at the church. Pastor had encouraged Shorty to assume that role of leadership, and made Eleventh Street open and available for his use. Shorty depended on Lyda in so many ways, and managing the grocery was just a part of what she did for him. If Lyda was sick, it was only right that Shorty leave after the main service to ensure that Lyda's needs were being met.

Pastor wondered if he had offended Shorty in some way, or perhaps embarrassed him. He surely had not intended any slight. Perhaps he should have spoken with Shorty before the service to let him know his thoughts. Pastor had concerns about unduly extending the length of the service. He knew Shorty wanted to speak, and a short, topical message may have been appropriate. The members might have enjoyed and appreciated a lesson by Shorty. He could talk in such a succinct and understandable manner. Shorty's talk probably would not have taken that long.

Pastor knew from experience that people could be easily offended. The slightest and most unintended word or deed could separate a friend for life. "Carrying their feelings on a sleeve," he had heard it called. Pastor had not meant to offend Shorty, but still he felt bad. As he concluded the opening prayer, on behalf of all present, and especially for himself, he sought forgiveness from God, forgiveness for any word unspoken or deed not done.

13.

Intermission

Gail drove home from church. Even though it was Easter, she had enjoyed as much religion as she wanted for one day. Home was not far away, and the traffic was light. She made excellent time. Gail had perspired heavily during the church service. The heat and lack of circulating air made her almost nauseous.

She looked forward to a quick shower and change of clothes. Both would help relieve the discomfort of a sweaty, clinging dress. But as she disrobed, she realized that she did not have enough time for a shower. Anyway, a shower in this heat with no air conditioning might only make matters worse.

Completely uncovered, she slipped into one of Ron's sleeveless undershirts, thin and white. She wore no brassiere; it fit too tightly and the temperature was too high. She didn't want anything artificial to cling and pinch her flesh. Clean panties would do for now; just stand near the open kitchen window; seduce a gentle breeze to cool her; and wait.

She expected a knock on the back door – to hear a familiar voice, in an excited utterance say, "Special delivery for Gail. I'm here to fill your order." But there was no knock on the door; no sound except the leaves gently caressing each other outside the open window.

She was certain that her verbal innuendos had been understood, that her furtive glances warmly embraced. There had been nods and subtle movements of silent agreement. He should have been here by now.

Did she misinterpret his looks? She was experienced in these matters. She had orchestrated illicit sorties before. Ron was either blind or oblivious to her needs. She liked religion as much as anyone, but religion did not excite her like the touch of a strange hand.

He should have been here long ago. The church was not that far away. Time and opportunity were quickly passing. Ron would be home from church soon. Did he really understand the invitation, or did he just chicken out?

Gail had been stood up before. Wondering why Harold had not come, she wistfully recalled another failed liaison: same place, same result. Maybe Eleventh Street had been a jinx all along. It had been the site of the East Side Dance Hall, when she was attending the First Fellowship Baptist Church at the Five Points location. Why did the church have to move to Eleventh Street?

Ron would occasionally travel out of town for business meetings and conferences. One weekend, Ron was in Columbus doing his duty as a union delegate for the United Dairymen of America. He said that he would be gone the entire weekend, coming home Sunday afternoon or even later. He would ride with a fellow delegate, so Gail could have the car. The house would be empty, but Gail had resolved not to be alone.

For Gail, Ron's absence would also mean no church on Sunday morning, and definitely no church on Saturday night. Only later did she learn of the murder, and naturally, she had been shocked. But she had also been disappointed when the city later closed the dance hall at Eleventh Street and sold it to her church.

But on that Saturday night, she had danced with the man whom she later learned was the victim. Though she had danced with many men before, that night the victim had dominated her time on the dance floor. He had fixated his attention on her, and tried his best to sweet talk her out the door.

Gail was not above being seduced; but her conscience, such as it was, and Ron's work schedule, constrained her cheating to one man at a time. The victim would have been a good candidate, but the only reason she was at the dance hall that night was to meet another man.

The other man was from back home in Kentucky. A man who had made her feel like a real woman. A man she had thought about for weeks. And it was this man who said he'd be back in Hamilton that Saturday night.

The man was from Corbin. He knew many of the same people that Gail had known. He traveled a great deal with his job and said that he really liked Hamilton. He sold a lot of welding supplies to the local businesses. He said that he had been heartbroken since high school. He said that he had lost his true love to a cripple and had never really gotten over it. He was still looking for love. He told Gail that in her he had found it, and unlike in his timid youth, he was willing to fight to keep it. He made her tremble. He excited her.

But where was he? It was nearly midnight and he still hadn't arrived. She would have to leave soon, and she hoped that the man who had dominated her all night would leave first. But he didn't. He'd only stepped outside for a smoke.

When she heard the scream, she didn't know what had happened, but she knew it could not be good. She also knew she couldn't get caught in a dance hall, and certainly not at this hour of the night. So she slipped out the back door when all the patrons rushed to the front to witness the commotion. She got in her car and headed home.

There was no one on the streets, no traffic to slow her journey home. But she did remember seeing a man walking in the shadows on Main Street. He seemed to be in a hurry, and he seemed to be talking to himself. She had always wondered if the man could identify her.

The flashback was a painful reminder of how close she had been to disaster. Disaster as in murder, and certainly, disaster as to her marriage. Ron would have found her out and Ron would not have understood. So when Harold didn't show (she couldn't bring herself to call him "Shorty"), she relaxed.

She should have known better. Nothing good ever come to her out of Eleventh Street. Though they had converted the old dance hall to a church, nothing changed for Gail. It was the same place and the same result. She had been jilted … again.

Being an unfaithful wife was becoming a more difficult task with each passing year. Her good looks would not last forever. As she headed to the bathroom to undress and shower, she wondered if her lust would subside at the same rate as her feminine features. Taking a longer look in the full-length mirror than usual, she hoped that it would.

14.

Communion

The communion service concluded after about thirty minutes. Pastor offered another short prayer and verse of scripture before the unleavened bread was served, and again before the grape juice. Maggie had helped prepare the unleavened bread. Lizzy, Pastor's wife, patiently led her through the process. No yeast, just the dough flattened level, about a quarter-inch thick. Baked in the oven at four hundred and fifty degrees for twenty minutes. *Voila*! Unleavened bread. Just like the bread Jesus used at His last supper.

The tray of unleavened bread was pale white in color, sliced with a kitchen knife into smaller pieces, each about one-half inch square. The pieces were placed into two silver bowls. One bowl for the women; one bowl for the men. As the bowl was passed, each person took a piece of bread, held it in their hand, and continued to pass the bowl to the next person. The women participating in the communion service slightly outnumbered the men, so the men finished first and waited patiently for each woman to receive her portion of the bread.

After the last person had taken their slice from the silver bowl, Lizzy proceeded to retrieve the bowl from her side of the aisle, and Jerry Sullivant did likewise for the men. Then Pastor stood and said, "As Jesus told his disciples, take and eat: this is my body." Each participant then placed the unleavened bread to their mouth and did as Pastor said.

Lizzy and Sister Lawrence had already poured the grape juice into the two large, ornate cups. It was time for the second part of the communion service. This time, Pastor did not wait. Before the first sip was taken, he paraphrased scripture again by saying, "Drink, for this is my blood. The blood of the new testament which is shed for many, for the remission of sins."

As the cups were passed on both sides of the aisle, the lips of each woman and each man touched their respective cup. There was no thought given to whether the one-cup procedure was sanitary or not. One cup had always been the method; one cup is all that Jesus used at the Last Supper.

Other churches may have switched to multiple, smaller cups on a circular serving tray, but as the words of a song then popular proclaimed, "If it was good enough for Paul and Silas, it's good enough for me." Most people who echoed that sentiment didn't realize that Paul and Silas were not in attendance at the Last Supper. Neither were they at the foot washing, which was the next scheduled ordinance.

The men and women were already in their respective and segregated pews. On the women's side, Lizzy poured water from a beautiful white pitcher into a large porcelain basin. Then, she took a long white linen cloth and wrapped it around her waist. She draped the excess length over her shoulder. Bending down and then resting on both knees, she proceeded to wash the feet of Sister Lawrence, gently moving the lukewarm water over her arthritic toes and ankles. She lifted her feet out of the water and began to wipe them dry with the linen cloth draped from her shoulder. Sister Lawrence sat silently and very still as she watched Lizzy carefully lift her feet from the basin. They both stood and embraced each other. There were tears in both their eyes.

Lizzy took off the linen cloth and helped Sister Lawrence arrange it in the same manner as she had done. Sister Lawrence turned to face the woman sitting next to her. Ben Langley's wife, Edith, was waiting, her shoes and hose already removed. Sister Lawrence kneeled, as best she could with Lizzy's help, and started to wash the feet of her sister in Christ.

On the men's side of the aisle, the process was virtually identical. Pastor had initiated the service by washing the feet of Jerry Sullivant. Jerry was the senior deacon, and as such, he washed the feet of two people in the service. After Pastor had washed Jerry's feet and Jerry his, Jerry then proceeded to wash the feet of the man seated next to him. Each man in turn washed the feet of the next man seated on the pew. As the feet of the last man in the front pew were washed, the men would exit, leaving the entire front pew empty for the next group of men to enter and perform their service for each other.

The men still remaining after the communion service sat in pews several rows back, until it was their turn to move to the front pew. Often fathers would sit next to their son or best friend, intentionally staging the order so as to be sure that their feet were washed by someone they loved and trusted. Many felt more comfortable washing the feet of a friend or loved one, as opposed to performing the ritual with someone of only casual acquaintance.

Lucas was a relatively new member. Though liked by all, he did not yet have any one person in the church he could truly call a friend, except Pastor. If anyone in the church held a special place in his heart, it was Pastor.

It was Pastor who had left the pulpit and walked back up the aisle to the front door where Lucas knelt crying. Only by mistake had Lucas entered that door the first time. But later, on a different day, at the same door, Lucas had finally found a home. Today would be a solemn reminder that he needed a continual cleansing. Lucas knew that he walked in a sinful world. If the Apostle Paul had not already claimed the honor, Lucas believed that he was worthy to be called the "chief of sinners." He reflected on today's sermon when Pastor talked about Peter at the last supper, and paraphrased what Peter had said to Jesus, "Don't just wash my feet, Lord; wash me all over."

It was Lucas's turn to approach the front row to remove his shoes and socks. As he sat down, he felt a nudge from Fred Meadows. Lucas felt a sigh of relief. Fred would wash the feet of Lucas. His eyes started to water over, but he blinked repeatedly, holding back the tears. His body began to shiver just a bit, but maybe he could blame the mild quaking on the cool water in the basin. There was nothing to cry about, but his life was so different now. So wonderfully different, clean and new.

He looked over to his left, across the aisle where the women were seated. He saw Maggie undraping the linen cloth from her waist, and helping the woman next to her prepare to wash the feet of another. What used to bore him to tears now brought tears of joy. Fred knelt on sore knees, and with rough and callused hands, gently covered the sores on Lucas's feet with water. Lucas began to silently hum the words, "What a friend we have in Jesus; all our sins and griefs to bear."

Shorty silently slipped into the pew next to Lucas. He was late to the service, but Lyda was feeling better and had encouraged him to return to church. Shorty had many faults, and had faced many a trial, but over the years he had learned that with each temptation, the Lord provided a means of escape. Today, his escape was to sit humbly as Lucas began to awkwardly wash his feet – feet that had been tempted to stray from the fold, but feet that now rested in a basin of cool water. His feet were bare and exposed. He had nothing to hide; nothing to regret.

15.

Decision

Pastor may have looked like Moses, but he would never live as long as Moses. As he approached his mid-sixties, physical ailments and years of hard labor had taken their toll on his body. It was becoming more difficult for him to manage steps and stairwells. Once seated, he rose with considerable strain. His eyesight was failing, and even though he now wore glasses, they kept sliding down his nose when he lowered his head to reference scripture as he preached. He said he was tired, and that maybe the church needed a younger man. A man with more energy to lead them into the next phase. He needed a Joshua to succeed him. He wondered if Shorty would be up to the task.

Eleventh Street Baptist had outgrown the dance hall, and the facility was in a poor state of repair. Renovation was not financially feasible; the building would have to be razed to the ground and replaced with a brand-new and functional sanctuary. The church needed classrooms, a kitchen, and all the features being made available in other churches intent on growing and meeting the needs of their members. Pastor envisioned a basement and a balcony, both of which would add more classrooms and seats for new members.

The members were giving money faithfully, regularly and abundantly. The church had enough cash to demolish the dance hall and build the facility that Pastor often dreamed and spoke about. But Pastor also wanted an indoor baptismal pool, a place inside the church and behind the pulpit where new converts could be baptized.

This architectural concept caused much consternation among the more senior members of the church. They had been baptized in a river or pond or lake, just as the baptisms of old were performed. Baptism was a sacred ordinance, and strict adherence to biblical principles was absolutely required. Why change now?

Eleventh Street had always gone to the Little Miami River to perform the baptisms of its new members. The river was clean and the location safe; no one had gotten sick or drowned yet. Such a concept was a slippery theological slope, they argued. The concept was just what the Apostle Paul had warned in his writings: "Beware of strange doctrine."

Pastor understood their concerns, but did not agree. Baptisms were often canceled or postponed because of cold or inclement weather. Most members of the church either failed or refused to attend, because the drive from the church to the river took too long and there was not enough parking on the side of the road or near the baptismal site.

"Did the Philippian jailer get baptized in a river?" Pastor would ask. "Did Peter baptize Cornelius in the Mediterranean Sea?"

Although they had no ready or plausible answer to Pastor's questions, they took some comfort in knowing that at least these named by Pastor had not been sprinkled. At least they thought that was the case.

Wednesday services were being attended with ever-increasing numbers. The new members of Eleventh Street, and especially the younger families, were attending with great regularity. Shorty's sermons were instructional and inspiring. They were an intellectual exercise in biblical teaching, and he delivered them concisely, point by point. He encouraged the congregation to bring their Bibles and take notes, and most unusually, to ask questions after he had concluded his talk.

Because of the time and effort Shorty expended for the Wednesday night service, he seldom attended the Saturday night meeting. Many members also skipped the service, complaining that it was too much trouble to rouse the kids and come so soon again the next morning.

Shorty was now sitting on the side pew, the "want-to-be" preacher's pew, for the Sunday morning and Sunday night services. Pastor called upon him to speak more and more frequently. Often, Pastor let Shorty lead all the Sunday services, morning and evening, from start to finish. Shorty was in his element and the membership was growing, not only in number but in true appreciation for how Shorty conducted the service, and the manner in which he taught them from the Word.

Shorty's view on scripture carried a lot of weight. If he had an opinion on the indoor baptismal pool, it could either unify or divide the church body. Shorty had said nothing about the concept, but Pastor knew Shorty had an opinion. He feared that Shorty's view might not be the same as his.

In any event, baptismal pool or not, a decision had to be made about whether or not to repair the dance hall or tear it down and build anew. Other options had been mentioned, such as moving to a different part of town, but they had met with staunch resistance. The church was "busting at the seams," as Wilbur liked to say, and there was no room for more folding chairs. Whether it was "busting" or bursting," it didn't matter. It was time to either grow or wither. Without a decision soon, the church was going to splinter and die.

Pastor knew that the time for a decision was drawing near. He planned to address the matter at the next regularly called business meeting. But first, he wanted to know what Lucas thought. He had gone over the matter many times before with Lucas, but Lucas had never said anything either for or against the idea.

Pastor explained again his concept of the baptismal pool, and how it would be positioned. Unlike the present facility, with a small stage serving as a pulpit, the new building would have an elevated area for the pulpit, which would be large enough to seat several people. By having the leaders of the worship service seated with Pastor, the side pews could be eliminated and the anxiety of not knowing who would be called upon to preach could be abated.

Behind the leadership area and pulpit, Pastor wanted a set of elevated pews for a choir. The church loved to sing, and had some talented musicians as members. If these talented musicians were given the opportunity, the choir could truly inspire the worship service and serve as a teaching guide to the congregation for new songs and hymns.

And then, Pastor said, even higher and behind the choir pews would be the baptismal pool. A small glass pane would separate it from the choir, and it would have a beautiful, hand-painted scene on the very back wall. People could sit in their pew and observe the entire baptismal service without ever leaving their seat or fearing bad weather. The person being baptized would not be put to the torturous test of cold-water survival. The freezing temperature and rapid currents of the Little Miami River could be reserved for its natural inhabitants.

Lucas had sat in Pastor's kitchen many a night after work, as Pastor had unfolded the concept from his mind into words. He had studied the blueprints that Pastor had borrowed. With pencil in hand, Lucas had drawn lines, circles and boxes; arrows pointing in all directions with handwritten notes at the bottom of each page of the drawings. Then one night, after hearing Pastor's passionate plea once more, Lucas said, "Pastor, I think I can build it."

Jerry Sullivant called the business meeting to order. It was a Sunday night and the building was full. It seemed as though every member of the church had heard what was on the agenda and nearly every one of them wanted to make a statement, or even a small speech, about the matter.

Pastor was not feeling well, and it was clearly visible in his appearance. His face appeared about to burst. It was his blood pressure, no doubt, a problem he'd had for several years. Shorty sat in the side pew as usual, and several new members stood over him, whispering and gesturing as if they were pleading a special and private cause of action. Shorty would only nod and mutter a brief reply.

Ben motioned for Lucas to come up front, because Jerry Sullivant wanted him to explain the construction plans for the baptismal pool. Fred Meadows had helped Lucas resolve some of the technical, hands-on construction hurdles. The plans as drafted could be implemented at a very reasonable cost. However, cost could not be the issue tonight. The baptismal pool itself would nearly divide the church in two.

The meeting's agenda would be changed and overridden by a distraught and determined group of members. If a baptismal pool were placed in the new facility, they would leave the church. This vocal minority was led by Pastor's own brother, the same man who had been the primary force behind acquiring the old dance hall site on Eleventh Street. Hank Johnson and several others itemized their concerns, and made repeated references to the Bible. The indoor pool was just not scriptural, and Eleventh Street Baptist was making a serious error in judgment by proposing such a plan. The Bible did not sanction an indoor baptismal pool, and the Bible was their only guide. Their conscience dictated that they not be a party to such heresy.

Their argument against the indoor pool failed to convince the majority. In fact, it did not convince anyone. It only reinforced the feelings of a disgruntled few objecting to the plan. When Ben called for the question, it was time to vote.

Hank Johnson glared at Pastor and starred into his eyes. Neither said a word out loud, but a lifetime of history together reflected in their gaze. Hank's own brother, his own flesh and blood, his Bible study partner for over fifty years would not come to his defense, his version of scriptural baptism. Before the vote was even taken, Hank stood and turned on his heels, slipped out of the pew and headed for the door. He was gone. Nine others followed. The front door slammed shut.

Tonight in the spirit of Baptist tradition, embracing the fundamental principles of democratic rule, the membership would address the question:

"Will an indoor baptismal pool be constructed in the new facility?"

"All in favor, say 'aye.'"

There was one weak voice in the back that said "nay," but that was it. All the rest were in favor; all in agreement save a few. But that few included Pastor's only living relative, his only brother. Pastor recalled a verse in Proverbs: "A friend loveth at all times; and a brother is born for adversity."

Maybe Hank would reconsider. Maybe Pastor could change his mind. Who was more stubborn? Pastor or Hank? But Pastor knew the die had been cast. Hank had crossed the Rubicon, not the Jordan. Hank was gone. Pastor's fellow warrior and comrade in arms had vacated the battlefield. Pastor would now face a mighty battle without Hank's strength of will and encouragement. A new facility, baptismal pool or not, could well be the last challenge of Pastor's life.

IV.

"Precious in the sight of the Lord is the death of his saints."

(Psalms 116:15)

16.

Pastor Goes Home – 1953

Shorty read several Bible passages aloud as the membership settled in for the important, specially called business meeting. The Bible verses dealt with money, and being sure you had enough to finish a project. Previously, the church had voted unanimously to demolish the dance hall and build anew.

Lucas had been chosen to lead the construction of a new facility on the same site. The word "chosen" was not really the operable word. Lucas had been "drafted" by Pastor to build the new church building. Pastor had literally "laid hands" on Lucas at the specially called business meeting, and led the church in a prayer so powerfully delivered that everyone knew that Lucas had received a special anointing for the task.

Men in the congregation volunteered to help in the construction phase, doing whatever their skill set would permit or as Lucas might direct. The women would rotate providing the meals and delivering them to the job site. Lucas would start each day at seven in the morning and work until all the volunteer help went home in the evening, or midnight, whichever was later.

Inside the foyer of the new building would be an engraved bronze plaque in honor of Pastor. Pastor had been the first leader of the church, and one of its original founders. He had nurtured the church, and each member, with a firm but gentle hand. He had been selfless, never seeking fame or acclaim for his service, and he had never taken a salary or any compensation whatsoever from the coffers of the church. Pastor had been a mentor to younger men desiring to be of service in the Lord's work, and indeed, Pastor was like a father to the widows and members in need. He seemed as though he never slept, always visiting the sick either at the hospital or in their homes.

And Pastor could preach – oh, could he preach. When he stood at the pulpit, you could almost see the hand of God resting on his shoulder, urging Pastor on – "Preach, Pastor! Preach it!" You could almost hear an echo of the Holy Ghost in his throat. Pastor's booming voice almost shattered a window in the old dance hall, at least that's how Fred Meadows told the story.

But Fred had an imagination that any child of the church would envy. Still, he wasn't exaggerating all that much. You could hear Pastor all the way to East Avenue, and that was three blocks away. On a clear summer day with the windows open, he could be heard nearly five blocks away. Beer joints in the east end quit opening on Sunday because of Pastor. The loud sermons disrupted the mood of their patrons.

But hard work, stress and loneliness finally caught up with Pastor, and he knew the end of his time here on Earth was drawing nigh. And that's the primary reason he had nominated Shorty to be the interim leader of Eleventh Street.

The new church would have a baptistery, a pool elevated behind the choir loft and the pulpit. The baptismal pool had been a source of controversy among the congregation, especially the older members, who had personally been baptized in a river, pond or lake. The old hymn "Shall We Gather at the River" meant more than three-part harmony to these faithful old-timers, and some left the church to seek another place of worship that more closely conformed to their view of scripture. Pastor never got over those losses. He missed his brother very much.

But the overwhelming majority of the church voted for the indoor baptistery concept. It made practical sense. The manner in which the proposed construction was presented convinced everyone that it would be a beautiful addendum to the pulpit area. It would be a point of reckoning, a salient feature that would draw one's mind and heart toward the altar.

Shorty had justified the baptismal pool eloquently, using Old and New Testament scripture and examples. From either a construction or a biblical perspective, the baptismal pool was a workable and wonderful concept. It was soon forgotten that the baptistery had been Pastor's idea and suggestion. Many were taking credit for the idea. The events leading up to the business meeting had been so stressful that Pastor knew he had to bring Lucas and Shorty on board quickly.

A flurry of specially called business meetings were successfully conducted before today's meeting was called. Within days after making the final arrangements, Pastor had a debilitating stroke. He could no longer even speak, let alone preach.

During the demolition and construction phase, the church would congregate at Coolidge Elementary School. Coolidge was about ten blocks from the church. Those members who lived close by could still walk to church without undue hardship. For those who drove, ample parking was available. Coolidge's price for renting the space was negotiated by Ben Langley. The terms were never discussed. Coolidge may have charged nothing at all for the use of their facility, but it was generally understood and believed that Ben paid all the rent requested and paid it in advance.

Ben feared that he might die before construction was complete. Ben lived, but Pastor did not. He never lived to see the new Eleventh Street facility complete. He died at home with the framed picture of his beloved Lizzy lying on his chest.

Pastor's last sermon before his death had finally convinced the membership that a change in leadership was in order. Pastor had used Moses as his example, and how it came to pass that the Lord spoke unto Joshua. How fitting that Pastor used this passage of scripture to describe the manner by which he would voluntarily relinquish his role as spiritual leader of the church.

"Oh, I can see the land before me," he said.

And paraphrasing as he did so well, he continued. "But the Lord has said to me, 'I'm not going to let you cross over. You are not going on with your people to the land which I shall give them. It's time for you to come on home.'"

Multiple rounds of "Amen" sounded, not only from the amen corner, but from all over the church body. But each "Amen" was tearfully uttered as many began to weep, realizing that the man who had loved them despite their faults was stepping down. Even the children looked forlornly toward the altar. The man they thought might actually be Moses incarnate was saying goodbye. Everyone knew that they would soon be adrift, alone and in danger without the strong right hand of Pastor to guide and comfort them.

As the service drew to a close, Shorty rose to his feet and quoted from the book of Deuteronomy:

"And there arose not a prophet since in Israel like unto Moses, whom the Lord knew face to face."

And all the people said in unison: "Amen."

Then, they began to cry.

Pastor's death had been a shock to the entire church. He had been a tireless servant of the membership and seldom took a day off from his duties, but when his wife, Lizzy, suddenly passed away, he seemed adrift, like a boat without an oar.

Lizzy had always been waiting for him at home, ever ready to comfort and encourage him. The trials and tribulations of a church and its many members can weigh heavy on a man who truly cares for his flock, and Pastor truly cared. Lizzy prepared his food, put him to bed and laid out his clothes each morning. Pastor did not have a worry at all when at home. Lizzy took care of it all.

Her death left a vacuum in Pastor that no amount of preaching could fill. He had lost the source of his earthly inspiration, and as each day passed, he yearned more and more to join her in eternity.

Pastor would not have wanted a bronze plaque in his name placed in any building, and especially in the new church facility soon to be built. "Thou shalt not have any graven image before thee," Pastor might have argued. But he never got the chance.

The memory of Pastor would never be forgotten by those who knew him, and especially by those whom he pastored. No one ever fell asleep when Pastor preached. His voice, in private so soothing and gentle, boomed from the pulpit with the force of a cannon.

There were no microphones at the old Eleventh Street Baptist. Just strong lungs and thick vocal cords. Back in Kentucky as a youth, they say he could call home the cows for miles around, and when there were no cows to call, you could hear him practicing a sermon, standing in a valley as his voice echoed all round about.

Pastor would be missed, and his leadership difficult to replace. Shorty had vowed to do his best, but he acknowledged that no one could ever truly replace Pastor. He was unique; one of a kind; and now he was home, and at peace.

But it was time to cross the proverbial Jordan one more time. It was time to build anew. Pastor would have insisted.

Lucas supervised the demolition of the dance hall, and solicited volunteers from the church to salvage as much of the used lumber as they possibly could. Rusty nails were removed from more lumber than the volunteers of the church thought were needed. But Lucas was determined to salvage, save and re-use every square inch of material that still had a useful life.

"We'll use it for scaffolds and braces," he'd say; or "use it to frame the foundation to receive the concrete footers. We'll use it. Just keep pulling those nails."

He would bark orders like a First Sergeant, a position he reluctantly accepted after his second landing on the shores of New Guinea in the Pacific. Second Lieutenants were dropping in combat like flies at a church picnic. The enemy seemed to target leadership, and there was continuous and rapid promotion on the battlefield. Lucas repeatedly refused to accept an officer's commission, preferring to be counted among his fellow soldiers, and also to avoid wearing a bull's eye for the Japs to aim at with impunity.

After the bombing of Pearl Harbor, the island was on lockdown. No one changed location without the knowledge and approval of a superior officer. For those being deployed to face the Japanese, martial arts training was intensified. Hand-to-hand combat was anticipated when the enemy was encountered, and the training contemplated that the enemy would not surrender or acquiesce to prisoner-of-war status. The troops were reminded of this daily. The Japanese would fight to the death.

The New Guinea campaign confirmed the fury and intensity of the enemy. Leaving the beachhead with virtually no resistance, Lucas and his comrades-in-arms stepped into a jungle with so much foliage that he couldn't see the men on either side of him. The only sounds were heavy breathing and the crumple of brush under their feet. As if appearing from inside some invisible bush, the Japanese would suddenly be at their throats with knives and bayonets drawn, slashing, darting and thrusting the cold steel of death into as many U.S. Army troops as they could.

Lucas often had nightmares about those encounters. Swinging his own bayonet furiously and with wild abandon, his only thought was that of survival, not necessarily the death of his opponent. He inwardly feared and subconsciously knew that he may have wounded or even slain some of his own men – fellow soldiers who stood too close, and within reach of his bayonet, as he battled in isolation to live yet another day.

As First Sergeant, Lucas collected the dog tags and cataloged the names of the dead. He sometimes took those opportune times to write a letter to his own family back home, letting them know that he was still alive, doing well, and hoping to come home soon.

In one letter, Lucas said: "When a guy is far away from home as I am, the things left behind and ideals he hopes to pursue when he returns are uppermost in his mind. Those things constitute the reasons that we are here, and we are here to fight for and preserve that privilege. I'm here to fight for and preserve that privilege. I'm saying this to let you know that I am not downhearted about anything. My brothers and sisters are worth fighting for, and that makes me feel that I'm only doing my duty."

Lucas did more than his duty at the construction site. Within months, the new facility rose out of an excavated hole, revealing a functional basement, rising to a stunning steeple, standing over a new front door. This time, double doors. The balcony would be become a favorite place for the teenagers. Hundreds would be immersed in the baptismal pool. Lives would be changed and hearts softened. Pastor's legacy of love and compassion would continue – at least for a few more years.

Within a few months after occupying the new facility at Eleventh Street, Fred Lawrence was begging Lucas to assume the role of song leader. Fred could sing, but he couldn't read music, and if he hadn't heard the song before or didn't recognize the song's title, he was at a loss.

Growing up in Kentucky, the Marcum family had never had much in material things, but they always had a song. Lucas learned to read music from his sisters, at least well enough to move his vocal cords through the scales. Other members of the church could read music too. Some more proficient than Lucas were quick to help him learn new songs and master the "Do-Re-Mis" of gospel hymns. As Lucas undertook his duties as the official song leader, he was surprised, if not amazed, at how well the congregation could sing.

Within a few weeks, a group of men singing bass would gather closer together in the pews, as did women who could sing alto or soprano. A new member, Jane Pender, could play the piano. Before long, the congregation was harmonizing on every song. Even if you didn't care for the preaching service, people would stay after Sunday school to hear the congregation sing.

Pastor would have been proud. Shorty loved it. After singing and offering such beautiful sounds of praise, the people were primed and receptive to the message he had prepared.

With Shorty's blessing, Lucas regularly let young children sing a solo in front of the entire church on Sunday nights. Their parents would be petrified, fearing a legacy of humiliation, but older church members would bribe the children with money or make a promise of candy if they would perform. Sometimes a sister trio or a brother duet would reveal how just a little bit of practice at home on Sunday afternoon could improve the quality of a song.

Even if a child forgot the words, the congregation would be blessed. You never knew what would come out of the mouth of a five-year-old standing on the pulpit in front of one hundred people. At times, it was hilarious.

17.

Finding A Friend

Shorty and Lucas had met each other for the first time at the old Eleventh Street facility. There had been an instant connection. An invisible bond formed between them. Both were from the same part of Kentucky, and despite his nickname, Shorty was tall in intellect. Lucas had volunteered and joined the Army prior to the war, but Shorty had been denied.

Shorty wanted to serve, but he failed the physical exam. The Army couldn't fit him with a proper set of boots; his left foot and leg were slightly deformed. They feared he couldn't carry a heavy backpack, or climb or run as fast as might be required. But the bond that quickly appeared between the two men was a mutual desire to learn, especially to learn the Bible. Shorty had read and studied a great deal in his youth. He had attended and nearly graduated from the Pineville Preachers School. Lucas had only heard the Bible stories. Shorty was a gifted teacher, and Lucas soon became his eager student.

Lucas knew that some of the older members, the truly faithful and Bible-believing members, could not read. They had never read the Bible for themselves. Despite this handicap, they seemed to instinctively know if a passage of scripture was being read or quoted correctly. They had spent their entire life in church, prayer meetings and revivals. They might not have been able to read, but they knew the truth when they heard it and could spot an impostor almost immediately.

Lucas had learned a great deal by simply listening to these older and more experienced men, but he wanted more. He wanted to know what the Bible actually said, and where the Bible said it. Shorty was ready and more than willing to direct Lucas to the primary source of such knowledge.

"Got to read it, Lucas," Shorty admonished, "and read it every day." They outlined a program of reading the Bible that would, if faithfully followed, cover the Old Testament scriptures in six months and the New Testament in thirty days. If Lucas remained committed to the program, the Old Testament would be read two times in a year and the New Testament twelve times.

"Got to read it to know what's in it," Shorty would say, as he continued to encourage Lucas to more and more spiritual growth. And read it he did, each Sunday asking Shorty pointed questions about passages he did not understand.

Teaching scripture was quite different from preaching. Pastor had the gift of preaching. Even though Shorty could keep the attention of a congregation during a sermon, he was also a natural-born teacher. Shorty was pleased to know that Lucas was so involved with a daily study of scripture. He hoped that his studious spirit would become contagious, and spread through the whole church.

If Lucas continued to be faithful, both in attendance and by example, Shorty was determined to let Lucas participate in a Wednesday night Bible study and prayer service. The church needed a midweek service. Seven days without fellowship among believers was too long an interval.

And Lucas, well he might develop into a fine Sunday school teacher as well, perhaps of young adults or teenagers. They all looked up to Lucas, and rightfully so. He had been through hell and lived; he had survived. He was a walking example of the grace of God.

Lucas and Shorty had one other common bond between them. They both were secretly fighting demons from the past. Shorty had not yet fully recovered from his torrid affair and disastrous marriage with Shirley. It had been years, but it still tormented his thoughts. What a fool he had been to believe that she would truly want him for a husband. All she had wanted was legitimacy for the child she carried by another man. Jilted herself by the true father, she had deceived and seduced Shorty into an unholy union. The marriage would never have worked, he knew that for certain, but a divorce in Baptist circles was the kiss of death. They might let you serve as an usher, or teach a children's class, but to assume a position of real leadership in the Baptist Church required that a man "be blameless, the husband of one wife." Guilt still lingered. Shorty had not been blameless, but he hadn't been blamed, at least to this point. He had more than a divorce in his past to be sorry for, much more.

Despite his renewed commitment to scripture and to the church, he regularly chastised himself. He wished he had never met Shirley, and at times, wished that she had died in childbirth. Would he then be the husband of one wife? Perhaps, but he would not be blameless. No, he would not be blameless.

At Eleventh Street, no one knew about Shirley. Only Lyda and his own brothers had any knowledge of his moral failures, and they never spoke of it to him, or to anyone. They loved Shorty too much to shame or embarrass him. Shorty's failures were the product of youthful indiscretion, and Shirley had been a demon in disguise. Lyda seemed to love him even more after Shorty told her the torrid tale. His brothers carried a bit of resentment toward Shirley, the woman who nearly destroyed the older brother they so admired. But no one knew the extent of the resentment Shorty still bore in his memory, or the measures he had taken to resolve the embarrassment he still felt. Shorty had more than a failed marriage in his past. He had tried to get even with the past demons and to even get ahead. More than one could play the game of love.

The demons that haunted Lucas carried guns and machetes. They lurked in dense foliage, coiled and ready to strike in the darkness of night when Lucas lay sleeping. The nightmares of war; the horror of seeing the battle rage; the guilt of living when so many good men around him lay dying.

He dreamed of his own brothers in combat. Two had been killed in Europe, though both had made it through D-Day and lived to walk past the shores of

Normandy and through the hedgerows of France. Horace was shot by a sniper while walking with his troops en route to a French village. Marcus lasted until the winter of 1944, writing letters home to his sisters complaining of the food, the cold winter and the wet gear. Yet when it came time to fight, Marcus led his platoon with honor. He was gunned down protecting the wounded at the Battle of the Bulge.

Posthumous awards of the Purple Heart for both brothers, and eventually, the Silver Star for valor in combat to Marcus, did little to assuage the pain of the loss Lucas felt. Horace was his big brother, the oldest, and his protector as a child. Marcus was his closest brother in age, in looks and in spirit. In their youth, they were often misidentified or accused of being twins. Lucas was inconsolable upon hearing of their deaths, which he did not know about until after he had made it safely home from the war himself.

That was when Lucas had turned to the fermented remedies of which his own father so regularly partook. Lucas sought to escape the memories of war, just as his father sought to forget the tragic death of his wife, Lucas's mother. She had borne eleven children, and she'd died when Lucas was only eleven years of age. After years of fighting abroad, Lucas could finally understand why his own father had become so distant emotionally, and eventually physically absent. He was constantly leaving home, entrusting the care of the youngest children to Lucas and his sister, Sadie.

Alcohol numbed the senses, yet it brought no relief to the mind or to the memory of a painful loss. Alcohol had become the master of his father's daily life – and Lucas had resolved that he would be different. He would not become a slave to its false cry of relief.

Maggie had pointed Lucas toward the light, and at Eleventh Street, he would have the support and encouragement he needed to follow the light. The demons of nighttime made fewer and fewer visits to his dreams.

Eleventh Street Baptist continued to grow year after year, in both number and spirit. When the Rowling family joined the church, the membership increased substantially. Ken Rowling, his wife and seven children; Ron Rowling, his wife and five children; their older brother, Junior. They all joined the church one Sunday morning. It took over forty-five minutes for the congregation to line up and plod toward the altar to shake the hand of each Rowling family member.

The custom at Eleventh Street was to welcome each new member personally, immediately after they joined the church. The congregation formed a line down the outside aisles of each row of pews, and sometimes also in a line down the middle aisle. Meeting at the altar, the current members politely cut into each other's lines to greet the newest member of the church family.

Standing on the floor to the right of the altar and next to the piano, Lucas led the congregation in singing a hymn they would all know by heart. The songbooks had been left in the pews.

Junior Rowling placed himself between his two brothers. He seemed shy and didn't say a word in response to the warm greetings and firm handshakes that he and his entire family were receiving. He only nodded in agreement and smiled sheepishly. As the final person in line began to pass by the altar, Lucas put down his songbook and fell into line to shake their hands.

Lucas stopped in front of Ken and Ron to introduce himself by name. "This is Junior," Ken said to Lucas. "He's our older brother. He's a good worker, but he can't talk so good."

"Hello Junior, I'm Lucas," he said with a warm smile and a firm handshake. "Feel free to talk with me any time you want."

As Lucas walked away, Junior turned to Ken and Ron and mumbled, "Loo, I like Loo." Junior couldn't sound out the word "Lucas." Consonants were a problem, but he could and would forever after affectionately refer to the only man who called him by name that day as "Loo."

The winters in Hamilton could be brutally cold. At Eleventh Street, the new building was like an icebox before the basement furnace started cranking out enough heat to stop teeth from chattering. Shorty knew that Junior Rowling lived close by, and that in just a few short months, he had proved himself to be a faithful and trustworthy church member.

He entrusted Junior with a key to the front door, and asked if he would be willing to come early and turn on the furnace an hour before church service was scheduled to begin. Junior lived only a few blocks away and eagerly agreed to take on this important assignment. The furnace, though relatively new, was temperamental and often difficult to get started. Junior proved himself to be a mechanical genius. He couldn't explain how he'd done it, but Junior got the furnace started for every winter service. The furnace seemed to function better every time Junior knelt in front of it.

Instead of sitting in the pews with an overcoat and scarf still wrapped around their necks for half the service, people now shed their coats at the door. Ken Rowling said that Eleventh Street had been a lifesaver for Junior, but Junior had literally saved the church from freezing to death.

Junior also assumed another important job at the church. As Lucas led the congregation in song, he had a perfect view of every congregant, including his own son, Mark. Mark was now almost eight years old and full of energy. His cousins and friends at church did not enjoy the same degree of adult supervision as Mark was privileged to have. As a result, Mark was regularly entreated by Lucas to exit his current pew and proceed to the very front where Junior sat waiting.

Lucas performed the act of subtle solicitation gracefully, as he waved his arm like a baton, leading the church to the rhythm of a song. Most of the church did not pick up on the signal, but Mark understood. It was time to sit with Junior and behave. While they were together, Mark would help Junior find the right page in the hymnal for the next song called out by Lucas. Junior couldn't read or count, but he knew when Mark intentionally selected the wrong hymn number. Junior took his job seriously. Mark and Junior soon became fast friends.

Shorty had been ordained as an Elder of the church. The term "Elder" was Marvin's suggestion. Shorty still had a latent fear that an objection would be raised to the term "Pastor" or "Bishop" being ascribed to his office. To date, no one had ever mentioned or questioned his marital status, but the Eleventh Street membership had grown so rapidly that he was never sure if a new member, recently transplanted from Kentucky, might have heard about the sins of his youth. Despite his lingering fears of being exposed, Shorty continued to lead the church for every service.

Eleventh Street had more members born in Kentucky than many churches actually located in Kentucky did. Whenever a week-long revival was held, the visiting evangelist would be from Kentucky. Preachers from Laurel County and the region of Somerset often came to visit and observe. And a few came to spy. In less than five years after constructing a new building on the Eleventh Street location, the church was again bursting at its seams. Talk of a bigger facility at a different and more convenient location took hold of both the younger and older members alike.

The most vocal objections came from those who lived nearby and could walk to church, or ride a city bus. For these dear souls, a move to the other side of town would mark the end of faithful attendance – a casting aside; abandonment of their spiritual welfare.

The offerings and tithes filled the church treasury to the point where the cost of relocating became an achievable objective. Without ever announcing a building program or organizing a so-called building fund, the church had enough money to purchase twenty-five acres on the west side of Hamilton. With cash in hand and a voice vote of all in favor, the church acquired the site. God's hand had to be in it; even the seller's realtor gave his commission back to the church.

Who was to lead the church in this next and glorious venture? Shorty was getting feeble, and he publicly said so from the pulpit on more than one occasion. He was in favor of the project and the move, but he felt that the church needed a younger, more energetic man to take charge.

18.

The Conference

Spies from Kentucky infiltrated Eleventh Street.
They smelled an opportunity to advance one of their
own. With the memory of Pastor fading, and Shorty
publicly announcing his own fatigue, the church would
be looking for a new and permanent leader. The
Kentucky contingent needed a man who would continue
the church's generosity to the small missionary churches
around Laurel County and Somerset. Eleventh Street not
only gave money to support these smaller churches, but
they also volunteered time and labor, helping them build
additions to the existing facilities and even taking a
substantial role in remodeling a warehouse into a facility
for a Baptist seminary near Somerset.

It was important, vital even, to these interlopers,
that a man of like passion be named as the new leader
of Eleventh Street. Their visits to Hamilton became
more frequent, and their hints and suggestions of a
likely candidate, a successor to the pulpit, began to
spread throughout the church.

Unlike Pastor and Shorty, some of these men had
doctorate degrees and multiple initials, either preceding
or following their name. Important and prestigious-
sounding titles that indicated some sort of advanced –

or supernatural – theological knowledge, were part of the picture. How these men had obtained such lofty appellations, or where they had earned their advanced educational degrees, was never questioned. They were accepted for what they said they were: men of experience, intellect, wisdom and concern for the welfare of Eleventh Street. It never occurred to the members of Eleventh Street that one, or even more of the aspirants would be less than truthful, honorable men of God.

Leaders of Eleventh Street were invited to a Bible conference in Somerset, Kentucky. The ostensible purpose of the gathering was to train church leaders, develop programs for church development, and encourage – if not inspire – appropriate change for a more relevant church in society.

If the Apostle Paul trained and nurtured young Timothy at Ephesus, these experienced and wise elders of Kentucky, like Paul himself, felt an obligation to be of service to Eleventh Street, aiding them in this critical period of transition. Choosing a new leader, a new pastor if you will, is an important and daunting task. It is not one to be taken lightly, nor one to be made without sincere reflection. To act too quickly could be the biggest mistake a church could make.

"Lay hands suddenly on no man" became the constant theme. Attendance was not demanded, but enough groundwork had been laid by the infiltrators that the church body felt compelled to send a delegation.

Shorty was chosen to lead a group of six other men. Wives were invited, and virtually all enthusiastically agreed to go with their husbands. After all, if the Lord's work took them back home to Kentucky, who could say no to the will of God.

The Coal Creek Baptist Church of Somerset served as host. Several pastors from local Baptist bodies, entire deacon boards, and other power brokers of churches in the area were in attendance. The church auditorium was filled to capacity.

The Baptists of Kentucky had a rich heritage and could trace their history from the early 1800s. Some historians claimed that their history could be traced to the eldest son of the famous backwoodsman, Daniel Boone. The annals of Baptist lore were replete with stories and biographies of men who sacrificed wealth, and their own health, to advance the gospel among the good citizens in the Commonwealth of Kentucky. The Hamilton delegation felt comfortable and at home, for they too shared many of these same legacies. They even wondered whether Pastor would have been listed with the esteemed leaders of Kentucky, had he elected to remain in the Bluegrass State.

The conference was scheduled to commence on a Thursday at noon, and to conclude by Saturday at the same hour. Presentations and topics included suggestions for church growth and mission outreach. A detailed discussion about the need for Sunday school literature, and a coordinated study of the Bible, took most of the first afternoon.

Sunday school booklets for each age group had been considered by Eleventh Street for several years, but they had been rejected for fear that the theology and

Biblical analysis they contained would be slanted to the particular bias of their authors.

At Eleventh Street, each teacher was free to teach from any passage of scripture they preferred, but generally all of them began with the Book of Genesis and continued to include the rest of the Bible. Only the most knowledgeable and bold would venture into a study of the Book of Revelation.

The concluding sales pitch for the coordinated Sunday school literature program was centered on the Book of Revelation. No longer should this book be a complete mystery, the speaker proclaimed. Men of great learning and renown had found the key to unlock the meaning of its symbols to expose the hidden truths and warnings for our generation.

Scholars from the Dallas Theological Seminary had written extensively on the subject. Bibles were now being printed with subject chain references, annotations, historical data and brief expository sections. "The age of true understanding is upon us," he proclaimed.

Continuing, he said, "Both the Thompson Chain Reference Bible and the New Scofield Reference Bible are now readily available. These tools were used in conjunction with the new Sunday school literature. These materials could be the most important advancement in an understanding of scripture in our time."

Only a few at Eleventh Street knew about the Thompson Bible, but Shorty had read plenty about C.I. Scofield. The good Dr. Scofield had been married twice. He had two daughters by his first wife and had been divorced by her for failing to support them financially. Scofield had ignored his first family while he courted his future wife, all before a divorce was final. Not only did Scofield abandon his first wife and children and refuse to support them; he swindled, schemed and forged his way through most of Kansas before he took up preaching in Texas. Compared to this eminent scholar, Shorty was a saint. But Shorty said nothing.

Prophetic, end-of-time preaching was becoming a more prevalent and popular subject among the Baptists. If the thought of eternally burning in hell was not enough motivation to repent, surely the notion that Jesus could suddenly return and catch you right in the middle of your favorite sin should do the trick.

"The children need to know these things," he said in conclusion. "It is your duty to teach them these truths."

On Friday morning, the emphasis was on tithes and offerings. Each church needed a budget, and certain financial goals. The membership needed to know about their obligation to tithe – and to give even above the tithe. The church leaders needed a better salary and more benefits. Housing in a parsonage was no longer enough. Pastors should no longer be required to have a part-time job in the secular world. They should be afforded the opportunity to spend their entire working day in the service of the Lord. The speaker made his points with emphasis.

The Eleventh Street contingent listened intently and acknowledged that his arguments sounded good. The only problem was that Eleventh Street had never had a preacher on salary and did not even own a parsonage.

They wondered if these financial incentives would be a requirement for their next church leader.

In the afternoon and on into the evening, ordained ministers took control of the conference. Two sermons in the afternoon, two sermons after dinner that evening. Without exception, the messages were a source of inspiration to everyone in the auditorium – but Shorty sensed an underlying theme, a subliminal message being conveyed.

To Shorty, the unstated but clear directive was that for a church to grow and be an influence in its community, its leadership needed to be better equipped and blameless. Indeed, the church belonged to God, but it could never rise any higher than the true character of its leader. He had heard this theme before. It was the basic premise for the Pineville Mountain Preachers Bible School. He also thought that he recognized a face in the auditorium.

The last session of the conference took place on Saturday morning, when the sermons zeroed in on the conference's primary purpose. They wanted to create an association of like-minded Baptists. There would be strength in numbers, with enhanced resources to build new churches, expand the mission program, and provide a financial safety net for the smaller churches. Salaries for church leaders would rise, along with benefits such as health insurance and a retirement plan.

This association would not be like the Southern, or even the Northern Baptist Conventions, to which none of the churches attending belonged. It would be restricted in geographical scope, and limited to only those churches represented at the conference.

A majority affirmative vote by the membership of each church would be required to join the association. Then, only after the unanimous vote of the conference delegates, would the church seeking admission to the association be admitted.

Lucas and most of the other Eleventh Street delegation thought the ideas presented at the conference had merit and were worthy of consideration. With all the churches united in a common goal, everything that had been presented over the past few days could be achieved. Just how the membership at Eleventh Street would respond to the concept of a local association was not clear, but those with roots in Kentucky would probably be in favor.

The last sermon of the conference focused on church leadership, and unbeknownst to Shorty, he would be the object lesson for the message. John Harkness stepped out of the foyer where he had been sitting – if not hiding from the conference attendees – for the last session. He had arrived from Corbin in the late afternoon of the previous day. He had been the pastor at the Main Street Baptist Church for about ten years. After graduating from the Pineville Mountain Preachers Bible School, he had served in several smaller churches, but had gained a reputation as a "hellfire and brimstone" preacher.

Harkness was a popular evangelist at revivals throughout southeastern Kentucky. Before arriving, he had read the list of registered attendees. He immediately spotted the name of Harold Graber. This was the same name Harkness had searched for in the courthouse of every county where he had preached. He had finally found the name in the Whitely County Court House while serving as a pastor in Corbin. Harold Graber's name was in the Book of Divorces granted in 1933. To Harkness, being found in the Book of Divorces was same as having one's name obliterated from the Book of Life. Years ago he had smelled a "spiritual rat." Now, he had spotted its droppings.

Harkness was immaculately dressed, and he strode to the pulpit as if he owned it. He looked down at Shorty with disdain as he announced his Biblical text to be portions of I Timothy and Titus. Shorty immediately knew where Harkness was headed. Both passages dealt with the leadership criteria of a pastor. Shorty also remembered the face and the look.

Standing before him was the nemesis of his time at Pineville Mountain. As Shorty emotionally prepared himself, he knew that Harkness was not really his nemesis. He himself was a fraud. As the apostle Paul had once said, "For such are false apostles, deceitful workers, transforming themselves into the apostles of Christ."

Harkness looked confident as he opened his Bible. He then proceeded to expound on the qualifications required for a man who sought the office of Bishop, or in Baptist terminology, the office of Pastor. Working from the last of the qualifications listed to the first, he spoke of being a father, a father of well-behaved children, of being a teetotaler, "not given to wine," of being temperate, sober-minded, of good behavior, given to hospitality and apt to teach.

Shouts of "Amen" abounded as Harkness gathered emotional steam. Even Lucas, who rarely made a sound during a sermon, offered a hearty "Amen" to "the apt to teach" part of the sermon. He thought fondly of Shorty, and his unique gift of explaining scripture.

"Brothers and sisters," Harkness continued, "the Bible is clear on these points. If a man desires to be a bishop, that's a good thing. The man is wanting to do a good and noble work. But as I say, scripture is clear: "A bishop must be blameless, the husband of one wife."

There were a few scattered and sincere cries of "Amen" offered as encouragement to the minister as he wiped his lips with the handkerchief in his left hand, slowly raising his Bible with his right.

"This is what the Lord says, not me. If you are not the husband of just one wife, and brother, that means if you've ever been divorced, you ain't qualified to be a pastor, least not in this Baptist Church!"

Some of the men stood and began to clap. The applause became contagious, and within an instant, the entire auditorium had risen from their seat, slapping their hands together and shouting "Preach it, brother!" and "Don't stop now!"

And indeed, he did not stop. As the crowd returned to their seat, Harkness's face transformed into a mask of righteous resolve. He raised his Bible, one finger inserted to hold his place in scripture, and began to gently tap, then rhythmically beat the Bible's cover, looking straight at Shorty, who had not uttered a sound or made a move throughout the entire sermon.

He reminded them of King David and Bathsheba, David's sin of adultery, his deceit and lies, the cover-up and the murder. Everything committed in a vain attempt to hide and conceal the evil truth. No longer beating his Bible by hand, Harkness began to pummel his audience with words of disdain and righteous indignation. He was no longer speaking to the conference attendees, but railing at them.

"But thanks be unto God for Nathan the prophet, who had the courage to stand and face the King of Israel without fear or trepidation, knowing that God was on his side."

He pointed his finger in Shorty's general direction as he lowered his voice in a dramatic fashion. Slowly reaching and drawing out his conclusion, he took a deep breath, and with feigned sorrow in his eyes and a furrowed brow, he regurgitated a final verse of scripture: "And Nathan said to David, 'Thou art the man.'"

No one moved as Harkness tucked his Bible under his arm. He wiped his brow with the wet and wrinkled handkerchief, and made a painfully slow descent from the pulpit.

The Eleventh Street delegation was in a state of shock. Had this man just accused Shorty of adultery and murder? Has Shorty been divorced? What in the world is going on?

Lucas came immediately to Shorty's side and whispered, "It's time to go." As Lucas turned around, everyone from Hamilton stood, and without fanfare or a parting word, shuffled out of their pew and walked toward the exit.

Two older ministers, both leaders of the conference, followed quickly behind, urging the delegation to stay, not to be offended. They acknowledged that perhaps their appointed pit bull, the dear brother Harkness, may have gone a little too far afield, but his message was not to be taken personally. They pleaded with them to stay. They implored them to stop and reconsider. Others from the convention began to gather around.

But when Maggie saw that one of the men pleading with them to stay was also one of the first to stand and applaud during the message delivered by Harkness, the new-age version of Nathan the prophet, she stopped in her tracks and turned to face him. Her face was beet red with frustration and rising anger. With her piercing blue eyes drilling a hole directly to the man's soul, she said: "If you all would quit beating the Bible and just read it, we'd all be the better for it."

With that, the Eleventh Street delegation plodded to their cars for the trek back home. There was no more conversation among them. They all started their engines, all except Lucas. The trip back to Ohio would be a long one as they pondered what trials lay in store tomorrow. Shorty was scheduled to preach the morning service.

Lucas continued to hesitate in his car. His temper was rising to a fevered pitch. The conference crowd lingered in the parking lot. Lucas grappled with both hands at the steering wheel as if physically restraining an inner emotional urge to bolt back out into the parking lot. He sat still and rigid, mentally counting the passing seconds. He slowly and with hesitation opened the door with his left hand. He quickly swung his left foot out and onto the pavement. He lifted his body upward and laterally, releasing his vise-like grip on the wheel. He was back out of the car and on the pavement. Both fists were clenched at his side. A dazed look clouded his eyes.

"Don't do it, Lucas, please don't go back." Maggie pleaded. "They're not worth it. Leave them be." If the crowd did not hear Maggie begging Lucas to stay near the car, they were deaf.

The half-crazed look on Lucas's face would have been enough to send a shudder through an angel. As for the scoundrels facing him, they more than shuddered. They nearly soiled their pants. One man turned to run so quickly that he slipped and fell on the asphalt. But he never quit churning his legs. He was determined to escape the wrath to come. He shredded his suit pants, leaving a gaping hole in both knees. Women reached for their children. The men knew better than to reach for anything. They had heard stories about Lucas's past.

The scene reminded Lucas of young Mark misbehaving after church, roughhousing with older and stronger boys. Tearing a new shirt or shredding a pair of pants while playing, only to face a good whipping upon his return to home. These men weren't boys, like Mark, but they needed a good whipping just the same. Lucas had no doubt it could be administered in short order. He had the experience. Right now, he had the desire.

Maggie's pleas continued. Lucas's dear friend had been pinched, and Lucas was flinching. The men who had just villainized his interim pastor deserved to be taught a real life lesson. Competing verses of scripture began to run through his mind. When the disciples knew that the temple guards were coming to arrest Jesus, didn't they ask if two swords were enough? Didn't Jesus tell them, "It is enough?"

Isn't there a time to stand for what is right? Isn't there a time to stand and fight? Must you always turn the other cheek? What about honor? Is it honorable to allow someone to impugn your integrity without redress?

As he mentally juggled the lessons of his life, he remembered a verse that Shorty himself had often repeated to Lucas:

"The discretion of a man deferreth his anger, and it is his glory to pass over a transgression."

As much as Lucas wanted to physically assault the entire flock of vultures that hovered before him, he drew in his breath, then relaxed his arms and fists. He got back into the car, and traveled back to Hamilton in silence.

Several miles down the road, Maggie lightly tapped a finger on her Bible as she looked at Lucas. He heard the gentle thumping sound and turned to catch her gaze. They nodded and weakly smiled at each other.

19.

The Transition

As Shorty sat in the back seat of Marvin's car, he realized that his days at Eleventh Street were numbered. He knew that he could not be the leader of Eleventh Street. The church was primed for a dramatic increase in membership, but his presence would stunt the growth it so richly deserved. He would be a stumbling block to the spiritual maturity the church so desperately needed. He had earnestly desired to be the next church leader and had diligently prepared himself for the task. Yet he knew that he had been living a lie. He had concealed the most regrettable events of his life from virtually everyone he knew. His secrets would cripple those he tried to serve. A cripple, crippling others.

Only those people he truly loved knew the truth. Those people were few in number, and it was only a partial truth. Shorty had never told anyone the whole truth. "The truth, the whole truth and nothing but the truth, so help me God"; the oath of a witness in a court of law. He had never been asked to swear such an oath, and he often wondered what he would say under the penalty of perjury. No one knew the whole story of his sordid past except those who had been participants.

And where were the participants? What would be their version? Who would be his accuser?

Marvin and Wilbur were his brothers. They were blood; they loved him unconditionally.

They never spoke of the past in a disparaging manner. Even Lyda loved him in spite of his failings, or least for the failings she knew about. But others in the church would not be so accepting or loving. They would view him as a usurper to the throne; a wolf in sheep's clothing; a devil in disguise. His attempts to lead would cause many to stumble. His teaching would fall on deaf ears. No matter how strategically he led or brilliantly he spoke, there would be suspicion of a hidden agenda. If he had hidden this one sin for so long, how many more sins were yet to be uncovered?

The conference speaker had been brutally candid. His public denouncement of Shorty's moral qualifications was unmistakable. Shorty was the object of his scorn, undeniably. Harkness may have been a fraud himself, the devil in disguise, but what hurt even more was that the young Nathan had been accurate in each allegation.

John Harkness had been senior pastor at the Baptist Church in Corbin for a number of years. He had continued his search for Shorty's past. By trial and error, he had finally struck gold. It had taken Harkness twenty years to strike full force, but the sting was fresh. He had been correct in each particular, righteous in each charge and convincing in his delivery. Yet he was wrong. Woefully wrong.

He had destroyed a man publicly without reservation or warning – but not without prodding or a reason to do so. The conference wanted Shorty disqualified, and Harkness was their instrument of destruction. As their chosen vessel, he may have poured out the venom with a heavy hand, but he had poured it where instructed. Eleventh Street would be looking outside of its own membership for its next leader. Hopefully, they would look to Kentucky. Harkness had been promised by the conference leaders that they would deflect that look in his direction.

If the conference leaders felt that Shorty was disqualified by the divorce of his youth, they should have approached him privately and prayerfully. They should have exhibited some of the same grace they constantly praised God for having extended to them.

But they did not. Shorty knew, deep in his soul, that he would not have compliantly received a private rebuke, no matter how gently and humbly given. His pride would have surfaced, and his shield of self-justification would have hardened.

Tears began to swell in his eyes. He asked God gain, for the ten thousandth time, to forgive him. To forgive him for his past lust and selfishness. To forgive him for seeking revenge. To forgive him for being a prideful man. To forgive him for being a secretive man. Shorty hoped that God had forgiven him. Shorty had surely asked enough times.

The Bible said that God would forgive him for all these things and more. But did Shorty really believe the promises of God? Or was he the hypocrite that Harkness had so graphically described? Shorty had been plagued with doubt, just like everyone, but he believed. Deep within his heart, he knew that he believed. He also knew that he had never forgiven himself. God was not the problem. He was.

It was time to face his own soul. To look into the mirror of his own heart and cast away the mask of self-righteousness. If he were to ever be a man of God, he would have to do as David did. Recalling the conference, and the message of the self-appointed prophet, Shorty would follow King David's example. He would publicly acknowledge his past. He would confess to the whole church body of Eleventh Street.

He would lie no more. He would do it tomorrow morning.

On Sunday morning, Lucas took up a hymnal and stepped to the front of the congregation. Attendance in Sunday school had nearly set a record, and it appeared that no one had left the building. In fact, the crowd continued to grow as ushers pulled out more folding chairs to provide a place for all to sit. They had already outgrown the new building. The singing was spirited and loud. It seemed as though everyone was making a joyful noise. The offering went smoothly, with ushers at each end of the pews, on both sides of the aisle, operating with unusual efficiency. The offering plates were brimming with checks, loose bills and envelopes filled with cash. The cool morning breeze through the open windows provided a welcome relief from the summer heat.

Lucas suspected that everyone in attendance had already heard about the Kentucky conference. He feared that they all knew how Shorty had been publicly shamed. He surveyed the crowd as he sang, trying to determine by a facial expression here or body language there that would reveal if anyone was in church for anything other than worship. He wondered if any had come for the sole purpose of further embarrassing and ridiculing Shorty. He worried and wondered, until he misspoke the words to a familiar hymn and temporarily lost his own composure.

Looking out into the sanctuary, he surveyed the older women and the young children. Despite the cool breeze, he could feel the fever of his own temper steadily rising. He should have been in a joyful mood, at least as joyful as the congregation appeared to sound. Yet Lucas's mind flashed back to the war, and to a jungle village where young, innocent native children, who had joyfully welcomed them during the daylight hours, killed his comrades with knives as they slept. Native women, who had smiled demurely upon their arrival, pushed slender bamboo shoots through unsuspecting ears around campfires, and fled into the jungle's darkness. No one could be trusted, he thought. No one.

Despite Shorty's past efforts at secrecy, more people than he realized knew of his prior marriage. Being the cuckolded spouse in a small Kentucky town was precious gossip. The news of his failed marriage spread like poisonous venom in the community, and as more and more families migrated to Hamilton, so did the story. Even Lucas had heard rumors and innuendos, but admonished the tale bearers to guard their tongue, and to judge not, lest they too be judged. Shorty had run from the problem, but he could not hide. He had tried to thwart the effects of a fundamental truth: "Be sure your sin will find you out."

Lucas had his own demons to deal with, and he also had some of the same doubts that Shorty had felt those many years ago. The love of a woman can cast a long shadow over reason. That which is obvious to others cannot be seen by the one stricken with Cupid's arrow. Love may be blind, but eventually the light of day reveals the true image of love's desire. Jealousy, insane and unjustified, can stand taller than reason. And Lucas had fallen prey to its power.

During the construction of the new building on Eleventh Street, Lucas had worked extremely long hours on the site. He rose early and returned home late at night. His relationship with Maggie was good, but during the course of building the church, it became more aloof, more like a business deal than a love affair.

Subcontractors often came to Lucas's home, seeking instructions for the next phase of construction or payment for the work already performed. As work on the church progressed, he came home later and later into the night. Seldom was Lucas at home when these instructions or payments were made. The brickmason, in particular, seemed to make visits more regularly than necessary. Maggie complained to Lucas, but Lucas really liked the man and encouraged Maggie to be patient. The church would soon be finished, and they would resume a more normal home life and schedule together.

When the new structure at Eleventh Street had been completed, Maggie announced to Lucas that she was pregnant. His initial elation quickly spiraled downward to suspicion. He tried to remember the infrequent moments of intimacy they had enjoyed over the previous months. He recalled the times when Maggie was tired upon his arrival home, or emotionally distant when he left for work the next morning. His mind slowly spun, vainly trying to catalogue the occasions, counting the weeks of physical separation, speculating and imagining, always imagining the worst. Had he too, like Shorty, been deceived?

The demons of war and the doubts of love flooded over Lucas as he finished leading the congregation in the last song before Shorty's sermon. The anger he felt leaving the Kentucky conference had settled into a knot of anxiety and fear. He knew that Shorty's days as leader of the church were over, and that the church would soon be in turmoil. He also knew that Shorty would be missed, and despite his failings, the church would feel a void.

Like Shorty, Lucas never spoke of his demons. But unlike Shorty, only Maggie knew of his doubts. The accusations he had hurled against her left an indelible mark of emotional pain that apology after apology would never erase. The child Maggie carried would look so much like Lucas that no one in their right mind could deny that Lucas was the father. The child even had the same physical deformity that Lucas bore without complaint. The sternum in his chest recessed rather than protruded. Shirtless, the child was nearly an identical replica of the father who had sired his birth.

Maggie named the child Michael, and Lucas did not object. He would remember the bitterness and strife that accompanied this child's birth. Maggie would remember Michael, the archangel. For it was Michael who contended with the devil as he disputed about the body of Moses. Michael was an appropriate name.

Lucas was ashamed of himself. He pleaded with Maggie to forgive him for the unfounded allegations he had made; for the baseless charges of unfaithfulness; and for the vicious language he had used to accuse and verbally abuse the woman he loved.

Despite the facts and the overwhelming evidence of Maggie's loyalty to Lucas, he often fell into a dark place of despair and doubt. His ultimate conclusion was that he, not Maggie, had been unfaithful. He, like Shorty, was not qualified to be a leader in the church.

Shorty took the pulpit and directed everyone to the same passage in Second Samuel that the minister in Kentucky had so effectively and dramatically used just a few short hours ago. Shorty acknowledged that he was not the pastor of the church, only an Elder. He reminded the congregation that he had been serving on a temporary and interim basis as their leader. He knew that the church needed some time to heal and reflect on who should be the next pastor, for there had been only one man to serve this church worthy of that title, and that man was Buck Johnson, the man known by all simply as "Pastor." Yes, Pastor, with a capital "P."

He reminded them of Pastor's last sermon and how he had told the congregation that they were about to enter a new era, a new period in the life of the church, as well as their own.

Now that the church needed a new building, a new leader was required. A leader who had been faithful throughout the wilderness journey. A man who had not feared the giants of Canaan. A man who had not sat down at the feet of Aaron's golden calf.

Yes, Eleventh Street needed a Joshua, but he, Harold "Shorty" Graber, was not the man. He could not lead them to the Promised Land. He was not the one God had called for this daunting adventure. He did not know the man that God had called for this journey, but he knew for sure that God's plan for this church would be revealed in due season.

"I am a sinner; a lowly sinner, saved only by the grace of God," he said. "My sins are many, both of commission and omission. Many of you may know, or think you know, my deepest and darkest secrets, but your knowledge of my past is not at issue. No one but God can know the whole truth, the whole story of my life. Because it is God who ordained my life, each step and each stumble."

He continued. "After Nathan the prophet publicly exposed King David's sin, please notice David's response in Chapter 12, Verse 13, where David said to Nathan: "I have sinned against the Lord." David later recalled this confrontation by the prophet in one of his Psalms, where he again acknowledged that this sin was against God, as he wrote "and against thee only have I sinned."

"All of you know one thing for certain. I have never maligned, or gossiped about, or belittled anyone in this church, or any of your family. I have loved you and tried to nourish you with the word of God. I have borne your burdens and sorrows as my own."

"But today, as much as we may love one another, God has a higher purpose and calling for this church than I am able to embrace. We already need a bigger building, and the site has been acquired. This morning I am asking the deacons to commence a search for the next pastor of this church. Your thoughts will be important, and you will need to prayerfully consider each recommendation and how it is given before speaking to the deacons. They may form a committee, I'm not sure how they will approach it, but the search must be diligent and covered with the prayers of each one of you."

"I've been honored to serve as your interim leader and can honestly say that each one of you has been a true blessing to me and my family. Quoting King David once more – as he passed the mantle of leadership to his son, Solomon – I, in like manner, say:

"Be strong and of good courage, and do it: fear not, nor be dismayed: for the Lord God, even my God, will be with thee; he will not fail thee, nor forsake thee, until thou hast finished all the work for the service of the house of the Lord."

"It is my prayer that God will bless each and every one assembled here today. Brother Lucas, will you lead us in another song as I close the service with the invitation? How about "Just as I Am"?

As Lucas stood, cleared his throat and asked the congregation to stand, Shorty gingerly walked down from the pulpit and knelt on one knee by the steps. Marvin, Wilbur, then Jerry Sullivant, and many more came to drape their arms on his shoulder, or to kneel beside and behind him.

Shorty was not the man Pastor had been. He was certainly not his equal in physical size and strength, or in force of personality. But Shorty proved on that Sunday morning that he was a better man than those who had laid siege to his character, and to his heartfelt desire to serve God and God's people. He had known for years that God had forgiven him. This morning, Shorty had forgiven himself.

20.

A Temporary Hope

The Mossy Creek Baptist Theological Seminary had just celebrated its first graduation class. Wilson Carey, a young man in his mid-thirties with a wife and two sons, walked across the makeshift stage to receive his diploma and a pat on the back by Dr. I.K. Ross, the seminary's president.

Dr. Isaiah Kenneth Ross was not a native of Kentucky, but had been instrumental in founding the Mossy Creek Baptist Seminary, located near Somerset. His quick wit and personality endeared him to everyone who met him. His charm and smooth manners disarmed any suspicion or reservation about his person or his purpose. He had no guile and was without pretense. Everyone admired and respected him.

He was also a true scholar. Ross had earned a doctorate degree at the Dallas Theological Seminary of Dallas, Texas, his home state. He had preached and taught throughout the South, and his presence at any assembly raised its stature and reputation. Ross was a staunch defender of the Baptist faith and tradition. He challenged the Southern Baptist Convention's view on church history, and wrote extensively about why the Baptists were not Protestants.

For these and many reasons more, many churches in Kentucky called him their adopted son. They adored a man who could articulate their views from the pulpit, and especially a man who could write with clarity and force in articles, books and pamphlets.

When the Southern Baptist Convention opined that Baptists had not existed denominationally throughout the centuries and that Baptists could not trace church succession back to the apostles, Ross went public with his treatise entitled "Baptist History Abandoned." He acknowledged that man could tamper with the record and change it, but tampering with the record could not change or alter the truth. "Men," he wrote, "may write or teach new interpretations of the historical record, but they must be justified by new and verifiable information." He charged that the Southern Baptist Convention had found no such new information and had ignored or suppressed the historical record to suit their own purpose.

Ross argued that the issue that separated Baptists from Protestants throughout the centuries had been the nature of the church. True Baptists held that the church had always been local in nature, and a visible body. Protestants, he contended, hold that the church is universal in nature, and as a result, invisible. Needless to say, Dr. I.K. Ross was not an invited speaker at the Southern Baptist Convention.

Theological fighting words peppered the various Baptist printing presses. Eleventh Street decided to adopt the good Dr. Ross as well. These Kentucky transplants loved nothing better than a good fight, be it spiritual or physical. So, when Dr. Ross spoke, the people listened.

Dr. Ross had recommended Wilson Carey for the pastorate at Eleventh Street. After two somewhat divided church votes, Carey was unanimously called to be the next pastor.

"Just get them through this turmoil and into the new church building." Dr. Ross advised Wilson. "You'll be back home in Somerset in no time flat."

The decision to call Wilson Carey had not been a smooth or easy process. Following Shorty's plan for input, several names were given to the deacons for consideration. In an effort to be fair and to overcome selfish preferences for one candidate over another, the church opened its pulpit to all comers.

Preachers, young and old, took charge of the Sunday services. Wednesday night services were led by the deacons. Preachers came from many of the smaller churches in and around Hamilton, but an equal number, if not more, traveled from counties all over Eastern Kentucky. It seemed as though everyone in Eleventh Street either had roots in Kentucky or knew of some promising young man living there.

I.K. Ross had diplomatically smoothed the ruffled feathers of the church's delegation to the Kentucky conference. He had talked with Shorty's brothers about the matter, he said, and encouraged them to arrange a private meeting with Shorty. Whether Dr. Ross was telling the whole truth or not, it really no longer mattered. Shorty had not only resigned as interim pastor, but he, Marvin and Wilbur had rented an old church building on Bordon Avenue. They had started their own church. Marvin announced that he too had been called to preach. He and Shorty were rotating their respective appearances in the pulpit. Marvin assumed the title of "Pastor" while Shorty reverted to the term "Elder."

The church that Shorty and his brothers organized started with just over fifteen members, significantly smaller than the three hundred-plus members still remaining at Eleventh Street. But these fifteen souls were special. Nearly all had been charter members of Eleventh Street, and every one, without exception, had been a friend to Lucas. Some had supervised young Mark during Pastor's long-winded sermons, doing their best to keep him quiet with chewing gum, or pencil and paper to draw, or by playing other inside-the-pew-type games for children. Even Jerry Sullivant left for Bordon Avenue. His Biblical prayers no longer echoed out the open windows of Eleventh Street.

On the first Wednesday of each month, the church gathered for a vote. Both men and women would speak in support of their favorite candidate for office. The deacons insisted that no one speak against a candidate; you were only allowed to praise and support. If you didn't agree, you were instructed to remain silent. No one would be criticized or defamed in the election process. If you couldn't say anything good, say nothing.

Lucas often said that "Silence can't be misquoted," but actions, even inaction, can be misinterpreted. The longer the process went on, the more nerves became frayed. Voting on two, sometimes three candidates, once a month, became a trying and stressful ordeal.

Not surprisingly, the church was relieved when I.K. Ross was invited to speak and to share his opinion about the credentials the new pastor should have. He dressed the part of a seminary president, drove a brand-new 1958 Cadillac and spoke with near-perfect English. He also taught a course on elocution at the seminary, and it was obvious that he was a master in the art of persuasion. Within a week, Wilson Carey stood in the pulpit of Eleventh Street. As he returned by car to Kentucky, the church voted to call him as their next pastor.

His first duty as Pastor: "Just get them through the turmoil."

Wilson Carey assumed his duties that summer with gracious enthusiasm. His gentle spirit and quick smile won the approval of each member, one by one. But that was part of the problem. One by one, before Wilson could meet and greet them, members were leaving the church.

Attendance dropped to below two hundred within a month, while Shorty's church steadily grew in number. Some of those departing Eleventh Street started their own church, meeting in a member's basement or a friend's garage. Men who had felt the call to preach made every effort to do just that, even if they had to build their own pulpit from scratch. They hadn't been insulted during the pastoral tryouts, but they hadn't been chosen. They knew that the days of sitting on a side pew at Eleventh Street and being invited to "say a few words" were over. They could not and would not be denied.

By Christmas of Wilson Carey's first year, the Eleventh Street church began to grow in number again. His sermons were not packed with emotion as were Pastor's, nor were they as deep theologically as Shorty's, but they were genuine and scripturally sound, and they called for action. The sermon always pointed the listener to some area of his life that could be improved, and it provided a tool to achieve the result envisioned.

The younger children began to pay attention during the sermon, and young adults began taking notes. Wilson preached in outline form, and it was easy for anyone to follow his train of thought. The following spring, Wilson conducted his own revival, preaching both sermons on Sunday and one each night for two consecutive weeks. Billy Graham would have been proud.

The number of people who came forward after each sermon continued to mount with each passing night, until on the last Saturday night, eighteen people walked the aisle professing their faith in Jesus. Even Jane Pender, the pianist for the last three years, left her piano stool to kneel at the altar. Who knew that a sinner could play those hymns so well? She was number eighteen. Young Mark barely beat her to the last open space. He was number seventeen that night.

Mark had been asking lots of questions. He had memorized the books of the Bible and had earned his own personal copy of the scripture. Like many of the adults, he was taking notes while Pastor Carey preached. He wondered if he was too young to be "lost." "Lost"? He wasn't sure. But he was old enough to know some things. He certainly regretted some of the things he had said and done.

He sat in the front row with Junior Rowling, but no longer as punishment for misbehaving with his cousins in the back of the church. He sat in the front pew now because Junior needed him. Junior needed Mark to find the right page in the hymnal when Lucas called out the title and page number of the next song. Mark needed to be in the front row to hear the gospel preached without distraction. Junior was not a distraction. Junior's innocence was an inspiration.

Mark enjoyed the discussions after church, quietly listening and intent. While the men dissected the sermon or delved into various passage of the Bible, he soon became aware of just how much his father knew about scripture. Sure, he had seen him read the Bible and sit attentively in church, but he had no idea of the hours Lucas had spent with Shorty in discussion and analysis.

Despite the knowledge his father seemed to possess, Mark had been troubled, and he worried about what it meant to be a believer in Jesus. What did it really mean to be a Christian? He knew how his father had joined the church; Maggie had told him the story. But Mark could also vividly remember one night when both Lucas and Maggie thought he was lying sound asleep.

Thoughts of the way his father spoke to his mother that night still made him tremble. Mark knew that his parents loved him, but if the temper and anger that Lucas held in check ever escaped, the exact outcome could not be predicted, but it could be imagined.

Lucas had threatened to leave Maggie that night because of something he said she had done. All Mark could remember was the loud and frightening voice of his father and the weeping and sobbing of his mother. Could a good Christian man leave his wife and child? And Maggie was pregnant, too!

For days afterward, Mark tried to console his mother. He voluntarily performed chores around the house that he had never done before. He helped wash the dirty clothes and mowed the lawn. He changed the sheets on the beds, washed and dried the dishes after supper. He was on his guard and best behavior when Lucas came home from work. Mark would be especially attentive. He became the dutiful son.

He never mentioned that night to his father. Whether it was out of fear or respect for their privacy, he would never determine. But certainly, Mark had no desire to be the object of Lucas's wrath.

As Mark continued to ponder and question his own salvation, he finally concluded that his life, and that of his mother, would be markedly worse if Lucas had not been saved. Being saved didn't mean an overnight change in personality, but it did mean an immediate conversion of attitude. And he knew that Lucas had begged for forgiveness. To forgive was only the right thing to do.

He had learned that much from the Bible.

V.

"In those days there was no king in Israel: every man did that which was right in his own eyes."

(Judges 21:25)

21.

The Audition

Wilson Carey had led Eleventh Street through the turmoil. The numerical growth of the church was now stable, at nearly four hundred people in the Sunday morning service. Once again, there was no room for more folding chairs. Many people were gathered outside near the open windows to hear him preach. This couldn't continue, especially in the winter months.

Blueprints had been drawn for the new structure on the west side of town, and everyone was excited about the prospect of a newer, bigger, more modern facility. A building fund was established and the people followed their hearts with their pocketbooks.

After three years at Eleventh Street, Wilson Carey had overseen growth and promoted a spirit of unity. Eleventh Street had even helped build a new facility for the Mossy Creek Baptist Institute and sponsored a missionary to Japan. Yes, Japan; former home to the Imperial Japanese Army. Lucas even seconded the motion to fund the trip.

But to undergo a protracted period of construction was more than Pastor Carey could endure. At the end of summer, he announced his departure. He would return to Somerset, and he needed to be there by fall in time for his children to enroll in school.

He was confident that the church would find the right man – in fact, a better man, to replace him. God had called him to Eleventh Street, and God was calling him home.

More than turmoil would follow Wilson Carey's last goodbye.

Lucas was devastated. He had grown to love and appreciate Brother Carey. His meek spirit and firm resolve, though in contrast to both Pastor and Shorty, brought direction and purpose to the church.

Brother Carey had had a distinguished military career in World War II, another stark difference between him, Pastor and Shorty. Pastor had been born in the 1800s, old enough to fight in World War I and to be Lucas's father. Shorty was also older than Lucas, and as time passed, he looked it. Lucas could relate to Brother Carey in ways that were not possible with the men who had preceded him.

Lucas and Wilson were nearly the same age. Only one year separated their year of birth. They'd both served in World War II. Lucas had fought on land. Carey was a pilot, flying at least twenty-five missions over enemy territory. They often compared mental notes and wondered aloud if Carey had ever dropped a bomb near Lucas.

Carey would joke and say: "Didn't you see me smile when I left you that huge divot on the beach to hide in? Without that gigantic hole, you would have never made it off the beach, Lucas. You owe me a few more shouts of 'Amen' in my next sermon."

Carey was very much like Lucas. He had survived the war, and though a victorious soldier, he had surrendered his life to Christ. He was a kind man, generous to a fault, but determined to return to Kentucky. He knew that Lucas could weather the storm to follow.

With blueprints now in hand, a site waiting for construction and a congregation eager to proceed, Eleventh Street had no pastor who would lead them to the new phase of their wilderness journey.

Wilson Carey left with no recommendation as to his successor. His only suggestion was to contact Dr. I.K. Ross. Older members resurrected their hope that men who had previously auditioned for the position might be given another opportunity. Many of the same spies from Kentucky returned, graciously offering their experience and wisdom as a new search for pastoral leadership was about to commence.

Tryouts for the job of pastor continued for months, and the local preachers came only because they were asked. None of them wanted the job. It was either a task too difficult or one they had been previously denied. Only the preachers from Kentucky were in serious contention.

During Wilson Carey's tenure, most of the Kentucky preachers now being considered were already familiar faces. They had either led Eleventh Street in a revival or served as a vacation substitute.

Each man had his own loyal following, and each man had a different set of strengths. One could preach with theological brilliance, another with conviction, and yet another with raw emotion. They all seemed capable, with enough experience and energy to oversee a growing church and supervise the construction of a new facility.

But vote after vote could not reach a majority for any one man. The church body began to tire, with certain groups bickering with other groups about who was the best candidate to ascend to the pulpit.

As though it was preordained by God Himself, Dr. I.K. Ross proposed a solution, a compromise candidate who might be willing to visit the church. And who knew? If it was God's will, he might want to come to Eleventh Street. The church just might want to call him as their next pastor.

There was only one way to find out. Extend an invitation. Within two weeks, with the church's promise to pay for his trip, Eleventh Street Baptist Church opened its doors to Dr. Israel David Rickett of Pine Bluff, Arkansas.

The church bulletin section of the Hamilton Journal announced his pending arrival: "The Reverend I.D. Rickett of Pine Bluff, Arkansas will be speaking this Sunday at Eleventh Street Baptist. Everyone is invited to attend."

The pews were filled to the brim; every folding chair taken. Lucas had been asked by the deacons to introduce Brother Rickett, and to that end, Lucas had met briefly with him before the service started.

Rickett had a bubbling personality, warm and engaging with a ready smile. He gave Lucas a firm handshake and a genuine "thank you" for asking him to visit.

Like Wilson Carey, Dr. I.D. Rickett was born in 1921 and had served in the military. Unlike Carey, who was a pilot, Rickett was a foot soldier. As he relayed his military experiences in the Pacific Theater to Lucas, his story of Army life glided out with rhythmic precision. At times, he waxed poetic. Sometimes he was precise in detail and provided painful, gruesome details. Yet, he was also pensively restrained in specifics.

Lucas was amazed that one man could survive the battles he described and still be standing to receive the multiple Bronze Stars he said had been awarded to him. Humbly, Rickett also added that a Purple Heart was part of his remarkable military career. Most remarkable of all was that Lucas had never heard of the battles in which he fought. Throughout the eloquent narrative, Rickett never mentioned illness, especially malaria. Lucas knew one thing for sure about the war in the Pacific. Malaria had felled more troops than the enemy. Rickett said that he hadn't been sick a day in his life.

He said he was a native of Arkansas and had met Dr. Ross while obtaining his doctorate degree at the Mossy Creek Baptist Institute. Lucas never mentioned that he and others from Eleventh Street had remodeled the old factory warehouse into the space the Institute now occupied. It was no doubt the same space in which Rickett had sat in quiet and prayerful study while in diligent pursuit of his next medal. And Rickett didn't mention why he had left Arkansas so quickly for Kentucky after attending a Baptist seminary in that state.

After being bombarded by the whirlwind recital of heroic exploits, Lucas couldn't think of anything to ask. Rickett asked if Lucas was ready to introduce him to the church and would Lucas support him as the new pastor.

Lucas would support whichever candidate the church chose to lead them. His primary concern was new construction. The building at Two Springs Drive would take his entire attention, energy and skill. Lucas had never built so large a structure before. The challenge would be monumental. In addition, the property at Eleventh Street had to be sold.

The realtor involved with Two Springs was optimistic, but pragmatic. The neighborhood around Eleventh Street had changed. A church structure nestled in a transforming residential area was not an ideal property in the current real estate market. It would take some time, the realtor said, but he would get the property sold and at a reasonably fair price. What was a reasonably fair price? The realtor said that the church might have to dramatically reduce their asking price if they wanted the property sold quickly.

After Rickett gave Lucas his brief biography, Lucas turned his focus to leading the congregation in several songs of praise.

Rickett sat in a chair on the pulpit, studiously inspecting his Bible with intermittent looks at the congregation. He would smile or point or silently laugh at some child misbehaving. He had won the hearts of almost everyone in attendance before he ever opened his mouth.

After Lucas's brief and polite introduction, Rickett took command of the service. He told a humorous story of his adventure in route to Eleventh Street, and before the laughter subsided, he delved into scripture with such passion that it caught nearly everyone off guard. His serious tone and precise elocution soon transformed, and mellowed into sorrow and inaudible moaning, as he related the story of a poor widow on her deathbed without friends, family or God at her side. His tears were real, and before long, many were weeping with him.

The invitation for sinners to come forward was accompanied by Lucas leading the congregation in the hymn, "Lord, I'm Coming Home." Nearly a third of the church came forward, repenting of sins committed while being a Christian or rededicating their life to faithful service in the Lord's work. For the first time in months, the church seemed to be in one accord.

Sunday night's performance was even better. It was the reverse sequence of the morning sermon. This time he began with a sad story, hit scripture hard, then told his joke. As the crowd laughed, he boldly stated that the next time he came to visit, he'd bring his work clothes and boots. He was ready to dig a hole. He was ready to build a new church.

And the church said: "Amen." All, that is, except Lucas. He couldn't put his finger on it, so to speak, but something wasn't right.

But what did he know? I.K. Ross had said that this man could do the job, and from all appearances, it seemed that he could. There was no doubt that he had won over the church. He had found favor with every faction. He could preach, he could laugh and he could cry. You couldn't ask for anything more from a Baptist preacher. The next church vote would be an overwhelming majority. Eleventh Street Baptist would call the Reverend I.D. Rickett as their next pastor.

22.

Old Neighbors, New Friends

The area around Eleventh Street had slowly transformed from an all-white, working-class neighborhood into a melting pot of older retired and young black families. City bus lines were available for all, but appreciated and used more by the elderly and retired. An elementary and a junior-high school were within walking distance for the children, and the neighborhood was still relatively safe and free of crime.

Neighbors spoke to and helped each other mow their small yards, wash out the trash cans or pick up leaves in the fall. As more black families moved into the area, it became obvious that they also needed a place to worship. Occasionally a black couple and their family would visit Eleventh Street. Their acts of worship set an example to the current members of the church. Many were reminded of the enthusiasm they once had, and how freely they used to praise and make a joyful noise to the Lord.

News of the church's plans to relocate and build became public knowledge in the neighborhood. The emotions were mixed. Some expressed sadness that a staple of their community would be leaving. Others were silently overjoyed at the prospect of being spared the inconvenience of cars parking in front of their house, blocking a driveway or otherwise disrupting a peaceful Sunday morning.

The black community, however, had another response. After church services on a Sunday evening, they asked for an opportunity to speak with the deacons. Their mission was to purchase the Eleventh Street facility and make it their own.

Not unlike the charter members of Eleventh Street, they too had formed as a small group of believers and began services in the home of their pastor, the Reverend James A. Stockton. From his home, they moved to an abandoned furniture store and through regular and faithful giving to their cause, they had raised a substantial amount of money. They were willing, able and ready to buy the land and building at Eleventh Street. They wanted to purchase every pew and fixture as well. If it was nailed to the wall or screwed to the floor, it would be part of the purchase price.

Eleventh Street had called I.D. Rickett to be the next pastor, but he wouldn't assume his duties for at least two months, maybe longer. He had not been a part of the planning process, either in acquiring the land at Two Springs or in drafting the blueprints for the new construction. He did not know the neighborhood, and the church would need funds to finish its new construction. And more importantly, who would want to buy a church building?

Time was of the essence, Reverend Stockton repeated. They had to have an answer soon. Their church was "bursting at the seams," he said, and he promised that they were going to move quickly. They would either move to Eleventh Street or to another location that many of his flock actually preferred.

Eleventh Street had some capital to begin construction, but they would certainly need more money to finish. It was easy to conclude that a buyer for the church would not be readily found on their own. Yet, by some random act of good fortune, here stood a group of men offering to buy the church, and pay a fair price to boot.

The deacons met. They announced a specially called business meeting to the church. Within a week of Reverend Stockton's offer, the church agreed to sell. Lucas suggested, and all agreed, that certain repairs should be made to the facility before they vacated and moved to Two Springs. The repairs would be minor and mainly cosmetic, but it was the right thing to do. As Lucas explained, "We would not want these brothers and sisters to think we were a bunch of slobs."

The Reverend Stockton proudly announced the acquisition and plans to relocate to his growing number of congregants. Many were skilled craftsmen, carpenters and masons. When the Reverend announced that Eleventh Street would also make the necessary building repairs to their future home, many of these men, without prodding or hesitation, suggested that they help the Eleventh Street membership in the construction of their new facility at Two Springs. "It would be the right thing to do," they said.

Spontaneously, a spirit of joy, praise and song erupted in the abandoned furniture store. The old piano was accompanied by an electric guitar, tambourines and a trumpet. The Old Testament temple choir couldn't have sounded any better.

"Get back Jordan, because we're going to cross over" became the oft-repeated refrain from the congregation. Indeed, they were going to cross over from a busy and dangerous site on the main route of Hamilton onto the dry land of Canaan. Eleventh Street Baptist would soon be the home of the AME Zion Church.

By spring, the church was ready to begin construction. Rickett called the Hamilton Journal and requested a photographer for the groundbreaking ceremony. It wasn't front-page news, but the ceremony did garner a headline above the picture of Rickett and the deacons, each with a shovel in hand, turning over the sod on Two Springs Drive. The article was well written and attributed much of the church's growth and success to its new pastor. The fact that he had only been there less than four months was not mentioned.

The church agreed to pay Lucas for his labor and leadership of the construction. Who could expect him to work without compensation? He had a family, financial obligations and mouths to feed. But as Rickett pointed out in the business meeting, Lucas would not want to get rich off the church, heavens no. He was sure the church could persuade him to accept, at the very least, minimum wage for his time. Eight hours a day, wasn't that a normal work day, he asked?

On motion duly seconded, the church voted to pay Lucas the minimum wage at $1.35 per hour for a maximum of eight hours per day. Lucas would give twelve hours of sweat, toil and tears each day for a period of nearly six months. In the summer, Mark worked those same hours in exchange for lunch, dinner and as much lemonade as was available.

Just as they did years earlier at the old Eleventh Street construction site, members joined the effort on their days off from regular jobs and after working hours during the week. The women brought lunch and supper to the job site.

The project was huge. The church bid out and hired subcontractors to pour the concrete, masons to lay the concrete blocks, roofers to pitch and tar the roof. Cranes with experienced operators were required to raise the arches for the auditorium, the undersides to be exposed, then stained and varnished. Carpet, tile, bathroom and kitchen fixtures were purchased and installed by skilled craftsmen, licensed plumbers and electricians. The heat and air conditioning cost was greater than expected, but the church was unanimous in their desire for air conditioning. They had endured enough summer heat in church to last a lifetime. Air conditioning was essential. They'd raise the extra money if required.

To finish the work, Lucas knew it would take at least six months of twelve-hour days, every day except Sunday. Every evening, the women of the church would bring supper to the construction site. Every evening except Wednesday, Rickett would give the blessing over the food and give thanks for the laborers, the weather and all the volunteers.

About midway through the construction, when the summer heat was at its peak, volunteer workers from the church began either leaving early or not showing up at all on Wednesday evenings. Attendance at Wednesday prayer service steadily increased, with new members joining the church at virtually every service.

Rickett praised those attending for their faithfulness and sacrificial giving. Without them, he said, the church could not afford the new sanctuary being constructed and certainly, without them, the new church could never reach its potential.

He bragged about how hard some of them had worked on the construction site and told humorous stories about how he had gotten blisters on his own hands while nailing down the subfloor to the Sunday school wing. Indeed, he too was a worker for the Lord, volunteering and giving of himself to the detriment of his own family. He almost cried when he told them how much he missed his study time, the precious time he needed to prepare his sermons, and the time he needed to visit the sick and homebound. Yes, he had sacrificed so much.

At the front door, shaking hands with the members as they exited Eleventh Street after the Wednesday night service, he would ask, almost at random, "Where's Lucas tonight?" or "Have you seen our deacons?" "I hope they're not sick."

Had it not been for the volunteers from the AME Zion Church, the construction of Two Springs would have taken several more weeks, if not months, to finish.

On Wednesday nights at Eleventh Street, a few of the Zion congregation presented themselves as guests, just there to visit and join with other believers in a study of God's word. They could also sense a rumbling of sorts, a subtle but effective undercurrent of distrust, if not disdain, coming from the pulpit. Exiting with the congregation, they too slowed to shake Rickett's hand and offer a hearty "Thank you for such a fine sermon." But they also heard the questions, and felt the tone of Rickett's voice, as he would innocently inquire about Lucas and other men of the church.

They were amazed at the high attendance, especially at the number of able-bodied men, clean shaven and casually dressed for church. The deadline to complete construction was now in view, and these men of Zion wanted Eleventh Street to be on time. A timely completion of Two Springs was crucial. Zion had already given notice of their intent to vacate the furniture store. If Eleventh Street was not empty and ready for their occupancy, a real mess was in the works for the AME Zion Church.

Craftsmen and carpenters from Zion knew where Lucas was on Wednesday evenings. He was at Two Springs with just a skeleton of a crew, and that was a generous description. He may have had enough bodies, but the factory workers, retired machinists and teenagers on the job were not qualified or experienced enough to be of any real assistance.

Without seeking the Reverend's consent, but knowing that he would wholeheartedly agree, the men of Zion began showing up at Two Springs on Wednesday afternoon. The pace of the masonry, electrical and plumbing phases of construction accelerated.

Even Lucas's spirit rose. He began barking orders like the old Army sergeant of years past, and the men of Zion loved it.

"We're going to build this church, Lucas," they would respond to an outwardly gruff bark. They had grown to know Lucas better than his own pastor did.

Reverend Stockton even joined the men one Wednesday evening. After observing Lucas exhibit his skills, and command the men willing to work, he said, "See a man who is skilled with his hands; that man will stand before kings."

Lucas heard him from afar and knew he was paraphrasing scripture. He couldn't recall exactly where it was in the Bible, maybe in Proverbs somewhere. But he recognized it when he heard it.

He thought of Shorty and the hours they had spent studying together. He missed Shorty. He missed Marvin, Wilbur and Jerry. He missed them all. But he knew they were in a better place at Bordon Avenue. They were happy, and they were worshipping God without the conflict and jealousies that were beginning to bubble up at Eleventh Street.

"Eleventh Street." It would take some time and practice to abandon and replace that name. "Two Springs"; saying "Two Springs Drive" had a different sound. The name certainly had more syllables, the site more acreage, and the building many more square feet. He prayed that the church itself would be filled with many more members as well. Yet, his stomach began to turn with anxiety. It couldn't be the food; he hadn't stopped to eat. God, he was thankful for the men of Zion. He just might make the deadline after all.

23.

The New Order

The church was finished and ready for occupancy in late November, just before the Thanksgiving holiday. The dedication ceremony was impressive, and attended by various local dignitaries, including the Mayor, the Chief of Building Codes and Inspection, and the Chief of Police.

I.K. Ross drove his new Cadillac to Two Springs and gave the dedication sermon for the new sanctuary. With microphones at the pulpit, and speakers anchored in each corner and at regular intervals among the exposed rafters, his voice boomed with a regal tone of authority. He vainly tried to compare the structure to Solomon's temple, but quickly regrouped and proceeded to laud and shower praises on the new pastor. The church had chosen well, he said. He could hardly wait to see what God had in store for the church.

Wilson Carey had been invited to the ceremony, but could not break away from an important and prior commitment. That's what Dr. Ross said from the pulpit. To the best of Lucas's information and belief, Brother Carey had no intention of attending. Wilson had told Lucas that one day he would give the reason.

At the first business meeting held in the new church, a motion was made to change the church's name from "Eleventh Street" to "Two Springs Baptist Church." A committee was formed to hire a lawyer and determine the advantages of becoming incorporated. In the ever-changing modern age, more and more people were filing lawsuits for slips and falls. The church could not afford to be taken advantage of. It was scriptural to protect the Lord's house with insurance and a corporate shield. Didn't Solomon have a temple guard armed and ready to defend God's house to the death? Indeed, he did, and Two Springs should too.

That was the gist of Rickett's lecture, and he mixed in a few tears of joy for the new edifice in which he now stood. The church approved his plan on a voice vote, without a motion or comment from anyone being permitted.

Robert's Rules of Order was not Rickett's forte, but it didn't matter. He had masterfully prepared for the business at hand and had brilliantly tutored his newest disciples to regurgitate his script almost verbatim.

Lucas had no objection to any of the business put before the church; he only wished that he had been given some prior notice. As chairman of the Deacon Board, he felt that the deacons should have had an opportunity to at least ask questions.

The legal committee was formed. Bev Langley, Jim Pender and Donald Dowling would be the incorporators and file a charter for the church in Columbus, the state capital. The charter synopsis read: "Two Springs Baptist

Church is an Ohio chartered church. The company's filing status is listed as active."

Rickett called his contact at the Hamilton Journal once again. With his picture prominently displayed, the article recapped a brief history of the church:

"Celebrating nearly thirty years of ministry in Hamilton," it said, "the church was organized September 1, 1939 as the First Fellowship Baptist Church under the authority of the Hazel Green Baptist Church of London, Kentucky. Buck Johnson, affectionately known simply as "Pastor," served as its first pastor. The church later moved to 555 Eleventh Street and became the Eleventh Street Baptist Church."

The article then proceeded to describe the church's move to Two Springs, its name change and the spacious facility it now occupied – a sanctuary seating nearly seven hundred, with a two-story educational building and gymnasium – all accomplished under the leadership of Dr. I.D. Rickett.

No mention of Brother Carey, and certainly no reference to Shorty. The plaque honoring Pastor had been taken from Eleventh Street and remounted in the lobby of Two Springs. Had it not been for the plaque and its visible reminder of a man called "Pastor," he would not have been mentioned in the newspaper article either.

The article also failed to mention how the church had grown at Eleventh Street, or that the original dilapidated dance hall had been demolished and replaced by a two-story educational building and sanctuary in 1953. No one would have understood, or even believed, that an indoor baptistery structure had cut an irreparable wound to the church body. At Two Springs, none of the new members knew these things, nor did they care to know. This was a new age, with a new facility and a new pastor. All things had passed away; all things had become new.

Within a few short months, the church belonged solely to Rickett. As the charter's synopsis had publicly announced, "The Company's filing status is listed as active." Rickett was indeed active. He would be anointed as the chairman of the board, president, secretary and treasurer of the new "company"; filling every position, if not personally, at least by proxy. The word "active" wasn't comprehensive enough to accurately describe the various roles that Rickett played. "You don't put new wine in old bottles," he said with a grin, as he made a motion to close the business meeting. "Hearing no objection, the motion is carried."

As winter approached, Lucas had no work. He had refused to accept opportunities to build a new home or undertake a remodel project all summer long and into the fall. His first priority had been to finish Two Springs.

Maggie's oldest sister had died while Two Springs was under construction, leaving Maggie a modest inheritance. Her sister had been a widow for several years and died without having any children. Her estate was divided in equal shares among her living siblings and Lucas. Lucas had installed an indoor bathroom and toilet for her years ago, all at his own expense. She was eternally grateful. Thirty yards to the outhouse in the dead of winter for an eighty-year-old woman was not an easy journey. Lucas had refused payment on each pilgrimage that he and Maggie had made to Corbin, Kentucky. "Honor widows that are widows indeed." That's what scripture said and that's what Lucas believed.

With Maggie's inheritance, Lucas and the family made it comfortably through a bitter and cold winter. Lucas even bought a new pickup truck to replace the one he and so many others had used and abused during construction of Two Springs. Despite the fact that he had no work for the winter, he appeared to be doing just fine with no apparent money problems. This, however, did not go unnoticed.

The church continued to grow in membership at Two Springs, but the sanctuary still appeared to be only half full. Seven hundred seats were over twice the capacity at Eleventh Street. The tall ceiling, exposed arches and vast expanse of the sanctuary emitted a cool atmosphere, an unnatural chill – a coolness not generated by the new air conditioning system.

The membership had also changed. Many had left Eleventh Street to join with Marvin and Shorty at Bordon Avenue. Others joined churches closer to their homes. The vacating members were either committed to Bordon Avenue's success or had decided to be a passive, if not invisible member of another church body.

There were also a substantial number who did neither, but who also stayed away from Two Springs. They were too stubborn to join another church and too set in their ways to accept Rickett as their pastor. While they were at home, their gossip and rumors began in earnest. They mocked Rickett's preaching style and his new entourage of followers, even sneering that he shaved under his armpits, just like a woman. Many of the rumors they started were viciously cruel and untrue, but it mattered little to those who were willing to listen. In their view, Rickett was organizing a cult of weak men and silly women whose sole purpose was to praise, if not idolize, his position as pastor.

Many of the rumormongers were either friends or family of Lucas. As the gossip leaked, it eventually became common knowledge that absentee members were intentionally causing division in the church. Their comments were unjustified, in poor taste, and mostly downright lies. At least that is what Rickett was privately informing his members. Before long, he said, he would publicly expose the hypocrites, every last one.

In the interim, Rickett proposed an expanded active deacon board. For years, the number of men serving at any one time had been limited to five. Rickett wanted twelve men on the board. "Twelve is a biblical number," he said. "There were twelve tribes of Israel and twelve apostles. The church is nearly twice the size it was," he continued. "I believe twelve is the proper number."

Without a second to the motion, if in fact he had made one, the proposal was approved by a voice vote of the entire church. The seven new deacons were handpicked by Rickett. They had all been members of Two Springs for less than one year.

Within weeks, the newly comprised deacon board announced that it had formed an audit committee. They drafted members with business backgrounds to serve, including one who had a bookkeeping service. Ostensibly, the committee would aid the pastor in formulating a budget for the church, and preparing one-, five- and ten-year plans for church growth. In view of the new facility, increased operating costs and a larger church staff, the objectives of the committee were unanimously endorsed by the church.

Of the original five deacons on the board, only Vernon Lawrence and Ken Rowling knew of or participated in the decision to form the audit committee. Lucas, Will Singleton and Al Bray knew nothing until the committee's very existence was announced. Will Singleton no longer chewed tobacco in the church sanctuary; otherwise, he would have choked on his own spittle.

Sunday school teachers were the next to be scrutinized. Being an able volunteer was no longer the only requirement. An interview by the pastor himself became the final determinant as to a teacher's qualifications. The interview consisted of basic questions about Bible knowledge and church theology.

Some of the questions were: "Do you believe God created the Earth or do you believe in evolution?" "Do you believe in a worldwide flood as described in Genesis?"

The interview could last ten minutes or as long as an hour.

"Do you believe in the virgin birth, atoning death, triumphant resurrection and coming of Jesus Christ?"

"Do you believe in heaven?"

"Do you believe in hell?"

Depending on the answer or quality of the verbal exchange, Rickett either gave his blessing for the applicant to assume a teaching position or encouraged the applicant to study the Bible more intently and to be faithful to hear each and every one of his sermons.

Without exception, the final question every applicant was asked was, "Do you support me as your pastor?"

Eager to please and willing to teach, the applicants fell in line. Without taking an oath, they pledged their loyalty to Rickett.

Lucas was not interviewed. Neither was he invited to teach the senior adults, as he had for the last ten years. Rickett said that the senior adults had so much knowledge and experience to share with the younger and newer members of the church that it was only right that their classes be combined. It would be selfish and shortsighted to isolate the seniors from the next generation of believers. The combined classes would be taught by John C. Carter, a recently baptized convert. Lucas would be welcome to attend the class, and he would. But he was tired; wearier than he had been in a long time.

Over a year had passed since Lucas had spoken with Shorty. He had often been tempted to attend Bordon Avenue to hear him preach, but his absence at Two Springs would not only be noticed, but critiqued. Rickett's sermons touched more and more on the unity of believers and the authority inherent in the pastorate.

"Thou shalt not muzzle the ox that treadeth out the corn" was a favorite quote of Rickett, and he got over a forty percent raise in salary when he preached that passage from 1 Timothy. He paraphrased the Apostle Paul by saying that elders who ruled well should be counted worthy of double honor. To Rickett that meant more money – a raise in his salary and benefits package.

Shorty agreed to meet privately with Lucas. "Bring your Bible," he said. Lucas began to share his fears for the church at Two Springs. Even more than the church, Lucas feared that his family would be irreparably scarred by the events unfolding at Rickett's hand. His family obviously included Maggie, Mark and Michael, but he had sisters, brothers, in-laws, nieces and nephews who were being affected as well.

They were discouraged and becoming bitter. He didn't know how to help them, to encourage them. He felt as though he was being intentionally ostracized from church participation, even from worship. He sat alone in the sanctuary, he said. Maggie was refusing to attend.

To give Lucas a well-deserved rest, Rickett suggested a new song leader, a "minister of music" as Rickett now called the position.

"Believe it or not," Lucas said, "it was a relief to lose that job." All he knew were the old hymns, but the younger members wanted newer, more upbeat music to sing. Lucas hoped that the young man now in charge would do well, even if it was Rickett's oldest son. He did have a good voice, and everyone seemed to like him.

Lucas had not realized it at first, but Shorty was not well. Physically, Shorty was failing in health. He had patiently listened to Lucas without interruption, except for an occasional nod in agreement or a smile at Lucas's humorous diversion to his tale of woe. But as Lucas finally gushed out the last words of his spiritual dilemma, he paused to look at Shorty, really look at him for the first time since they had sat down to talk.

"Are you all right, Shorty?" Lucas meekly asked. Shorty made several quick and abbreviated nods with his head and asked Lucas to open his Bible.

"Lucas," he said, "my time here on Earth is drawing to a close. For years I punished myself over the past, wondering what if this and what if that? Would it have made a difference in my life or in the lives of others? Without question, had I made different choices, I could have been the pastor at Eleventh Street. I could have been a respected colleague of every church and seminary here and in Kentucky. But I didn't make those choices, and you know what, Lucas? The Lord didn't abandon me. People may have, but God didn't."

"I can truly say, as did King David, "I've been young and now I'm old, but I have never seen God's children forsaken or his children begging bread." Lucas, I've finally learned not to look back. And this is what you must do, forget those things which are behind and press on, reach for those things which are still before you."

"Rickett is just jealous," Shorty continued. "You led the church when it didn't have a pastor. You encouraged the church to sell to Stockton's group, and you built the new sanctuary. Everyone in the church respects you, or least the members who know you do. Lucas, he doesn't teach, he intimidates. He doesn't build up, he tears down. Just stay in the scriptures. Keep fighting the good fight. Keep the faith. Stay humble, and the Lord will lift you up."

Lucas recognized the Bible passages that Shorty had so quickly paraphrased. "Read those verses again, Lucas. This whole thing is out of your control. Just press on. You've never been a quitter."

Later that evening, Lucas and Maggie had a long talk. Maggie had missed several services, refusing to go because of the way she felt Rickett was treating Lucas. Not only were his sermons a constant reaffirmation of his own authority, but he once regaled a story about a crooked builder, a man who did shoddy work and overcharged for his services.

How did he fit that into the sermon? Maggie had wondered to herself. But the comments had their intended effect. New members began to distance themselves from Lucas. Of course, Lucas didn't notice, but Maggie did. "Their wives," she said, "their wives are acting out exactly what their husbands have been told." "We're being shunned, Lucas," as she began to cry.

Lucas and Maggie had devoted most of their adult life to Eleventh Street. They had attended and given of their time and money. They had even given money they didn't have. She recalled the time, and it was more than one time, that Lucas had borrowed money to contribute to a building fund campaign or a seminary project or a mission venture. The only collateral they had to offer the banker was their furniture – the same furniture that Mark had walked on as a young child, scuffed with his cowboy boots and ridden like a bandit escaping Roy Rogers. It was worn out, and the banker knew it.

But the banker also knew where the borrowed money would be going. If a man would borrow to help his church, how could he say no?

They carefully discussed the thought of leaving Two Springs, but they both knew that, as Shorty had said, neither of them were quitters. If they were to leave the church, the church would have to run them off.

Little did they realize at the time how prophetic these words would ultimately become.

24.

The Audit

The audit committee had been asked to make a presentation at the next regularly scheduled business meeting. Rickett encouraged every member to be present, because there would be important announcements and recommendations made.

Ken Rowling, the committee chairman, presented a budget along with a long-range plan for church growth and activities. He also recommended a raise in salary for both the pastor and the minister of music. Every item on the agenda passed without objection.

"However," the chairman continued, "there is one item of business not on the agenda, an item of grave concern to our leadership and to each and every member." The tone of his voice and his serious demeanor caught everyone's immediate attention.

"We believe that there are serious inconsistences with the construction invoices. It appears that the church may have overpaid a number of vendors and subcontractors during the construction of our new facility. As chairman, I am asking for authority to hire a qualified accountant, or lawyer, to look into this matter: Do I hear a motion to that effect?"

A chorus of motions were made with an even larger number of people shouting "I second." There was no need for a vote in favor; nearly everyone had either tried to be the first to make the motion or the first to sound out a second.

Rickett stood well to the left of the pulpit as Ken Rowling called for questions.

"Who overcharged us? Who was supposed to monitor these things? How much money has it cost us? Who's responsible for this mess?" The questions kept coming at the chairman as he calmly repeated to every inquiry: "We're going to find out; we're going to find out; you can best believe; we're going to find out."

Lucas prayerfully thanked God that Maggie had stayed home with Mark and Michael. There were times that even he couldn't hold her down. She didn't take an insult with impunity – it was her Scottish heritage and Kentucky pride.

Maggie was standing in the driveway, waiting for Lucas to return home. She had already heard about the business meeting by telephone. The wife of a newly elected deacon had called. "Just wanted to let you know that we'll be watching you," the woman had told Maggie.

The independent accounting firm reviewed each invoice and called every vendor. They compared the prices paid by Two Springs to the prices charged to other contractors in the area during the same time frame.

The attorney hired to investigate had an undergraduate degree in engineering. He made calculations that involved price per square foot, price per yard of concrete, and the number of blocks and brick, not only delivered to the job site, but also actually laid in place. He also determined the lumber cost, which included the cost of subflooring, roofing, interior walls, doors and hardware. He, along with the accounting firm, estimated the true cost of all electrical and plumbing, wiring, fixtures and piping.

The first conclusion they came to was that Lucas had a valid claim for overtime. They concluded that the number of hours he submitted for payment each week was consistently less than forty hours. Yet they had learned, and adequately documented, that Lucas was regularly on the jobsite by 8:00 each morning and seldom left until that same hour in the evening, six days per week. The attorney's calculation suggested that Two Springs owed Lucas at least twenty thousand dollars in overtime and back pay.

The next conclusion was one that made no sense. With only one exception, each vendor and subcontractor involved with the construction of Two Springs had not only charged less than they did to other contractors, but they also had given a fifteen percent discount. It appeared to the accounting firm, which had many of the larger vendors as their clients, that their vendor clients sold much of the building materials for the church at their own cost or below.

During the audit process, they also managed to locate the original budget that Lucas had prepared for the church to approve while the church was still located at Eleventh Street. The actual cost of building Two

Springs came in substantially under budget, and it was completed over a month sooner than anticipated. Even the air conditioning cost, though not in the original budget, was included in the actual cost.

Reverend Stockton had found the budget documents and construction timeline in a desk at the Eleventh Street location. The lawyer that Two Springs had hired just happened to be the Reverend's lawyer as well. "Just thought you'd like to know," he said, as he dropped the budget in a sealed envelope onto his attorney's desk. "Lucas is a man of his word."

News of the business meeting spread quickly to the absentee members. Each family represented had volunteered their time to build and given money to fund the church at Two Springs. They had known Lucas for a long time, and no one imagined that Lucas would ever overcharge the church or secretly arrange for a kickback from a vendor or subcontractor. If the church was preparing to publicly accuse or file a lawsuit against Lucas, they had resolved to come to his aid and defense.

Rickett may have pinched Lucas, but the whole of old Eleventh Street, especially the Marcum family, flinched. Like Maggie, they were not inclined to take in an insult without a response.

"I met with the accountant this morning," Ken Rowling informed Rickett. "Well? What have we got on our favorite deacon?"

"Doesn't look promising," the chairman continued, as he tried to explain the intricacies of the audit, how everything was calculated, the vendors that were called, the conclusions they had reached. The more he tried to explain, the redder Rickett's face became. He had planted many a seed of suspicion throughout the membership, hoping that there would be a harvest of open disdain against Lucas.

"No theft, no kickbacks?" he pressed, seeking something he could use to publicly expose the man he feared to be a threat to his leadership.

Before Rickett had become pastor, the deacons conducted the Wednesday night services. This honor soon fell to Lucas as the Bible study leader for the entire church. Up to that point, most of the church only knew him as the song leader, a builder and a family man. Certainly, there were several who knew him much better, but the newer members often expressed to Rickett how much they enjoyed Lucas's teaching. Some would even remark, "He could have been a preacher, don't you think so, Dr. Rickett?"

A backstabbing scoundrel, that's what Rickett called Lucas behind his back – and the audit report had in no way changed his mind or his agenda.

"Tell the accountants to stop, and give them our heartfelt thanks," Rickett directed Rowling, "and by the way, there's no need for a formal written report. Just pick up all the invoices and bank statements and bring them back to the church. You know what to do, Brother Ken."

"But isn't there money missing," the chairman said. "Didn't you say there was a lot of money unaccounted for?"

"I'm not that good with numbers, Brother; let's just drop this thing for now and I'll get back with you. Now, don't forget, pick up every piece of information from the accountant."

"But the accountant, well I guess it was the lawyer, he said that the church actually owed Lucas money, a lot of money. What are we going to do about that?"

"Don't worry, Ken. Lucas will never sue the church. I bet he doesn't even have a clue."

25.

The Accusations

The new pickup truck was equipped with mounted tool boxes on both sides of the bed. On each side, crafted by Lucas, a professional-looking sign read: "Lucas Marcum, Builder: Homes of Prestige."

While at Two Springs to replace some door handles in the educational wing, Rickett saw the new truck and remembered how Lucas had gone without work all winter. No work should mean no pay. How could Lucas afford a new truck?

The audit report would not be written, and all of the data had been safely returned to Rickett's custody and control. Only Ken Rowling had any inkling of the audit conclusion, and he had been sworn to secrecy. How did Lucas get the money to buy that truck? These thoughts and more raced through Rickett's nimble mind. "I may have him after all," he mumbled to himself.

At service after service, Rickett either directly stated or implicitly implied that there were traitors to the Lord's work sitting in the congregation. He asked rhetorical questions such as "Where are my deacons? Why is our giving down? Why are certain members driving new cars and trucks?"

As he intensified his attack, he shifted his target to the wives of men he wanted to shame. "Can't they control their wives? Did you know that their gossip is spreading all over town? If a man cannot control his wife, he's not qualified to be a deacon," he would conclude.

With each set of rhetorical questions or subtle accusation, he read or paraphrased a passage from the Bible. After nearly one year in the new sanctuary at Two Springs, Rickett had multiplied his number of loyal supporters to a substantial majority. He had also discouraged or embarrassed most of the original Eleventh Street crowd so effectively that their attendance had become infrequent at best.

Maggie was furious. She had decided to be present at every service and to look Rickett directly in the eye for the duration of his entire sermon. Following Lucas's admonition, she seldom spoke, except to greet or say goodbye. But at the conclusion of each service, she would dutifully, if not defiantly, get in line with all those wishing to shake Rickett's hand as he stood in the lobby near the front door.

Lucas would sit in the second pew to the right, near the pulpit, the same seat he had occupied when he was the song leader. With as much energy as he could muster, he sang the unfamiliar praise songs. He stumbled over the words printed on the mimeographed sheet of paper that was distributed to each congregant as they entered the building. As Rickett preached, Lucas looked in his Bible, reading the passage cited by

Rickett, or the passage he should have used to put his message into a Biblical perspective.

After the service, unlike Maggie, Lucas would meet and greet other members sitting close by. But as the weeks passed, fewer and fewer people sat in his vicinity.

Sometimes Lucas would wonder, "What have I done?" as a newer member would turn his back to Lucas and walk in the opposite direction. Eventually, the only people Lucas spoke to were those who had been longtime members at Eleventh Street. Those who knew and loved Lucas were receiving the same cool treatment by the newer members, and by Rickett.

One time, as Lucas spoke with an old friend, he could see Rickett at the front door, whispering in the ear of one new member after another, while he pointed toward Lucas and his old friend standing in front of the pulpit.

"See, they won't even shake my hand," Rickett whispered. Time after time he repeated the refrain; planting the seed of suspicion, fertilizing the weeds of doubt; longing for a harvest of a ruined reputation.

Maggie was insulted at first. She later realized that the vague and obtuse questions being asked by some of the women at church were designed to frame a portrait of treason, an act of deceit on Lucas's part. Eventually she told the story of her eldest sister, and the modest inheritance that she and Lucas had received after her death. None of the newer members knew of Maggie's family, and her story was met with varying degrees of skepticism. The more Maggie tried to explain how she and Lucas had survived the last winter or had the resources to purchase a new truck, the more predisposed her audience became to believe the whispers of Rickett and his deacon board majority.

On the first Sunday night of November, almost a year to the very day after Two Springs's building dedication service, a specially called business meeting was announced. Every member was urged to attend. The very life and continued existence of the church was at stake. That's not exactly how the church bulletin read, but that was the underlying message, and it was vigorously reinforced by the conversation and chatter of the congregation.

"How could our church be in trouble?" they asked among themselves. "Who is trying to hurt us?" they wondered aloud. "Have you heard what Dr. Rickett told one of his deacons?" The seed had taken root; weeds were sprouting.

The Sunday evening service was scheduled to begin at seven o'clock, but the sanctuary was full at 6:30. When Lucas and Maggie arrived, they had to ask for people to scoot in and move closer together in order to accommodate them on a pew. The minister of music started the service promptly at 7:00 and led the congregation in only one song.

Without any further delay, since this meeting was far too important to be interrupted by an opening prayer, Rickett confidently strode to the pulpit.

"Open your Bibles to the book of Exodus, Chapter 32, and let us read at verse 26." He paused with dramatic effect, and then he read the verse out loud:

"Then Moses stood in the gate of the camp, and said, 'Who is on the Lord's side? Let him come unto me.' And all the sons of Levi gathered themselves together unto him."

"Brothers and sisters," he began, "this is the question before us tonight. Who is on the Lord's side?"

Rickett gave a brief overview of the passage and recounted how Moses had led the Hebrew children out of Egypt, across the Red Sea and to Mount Sinai. But before they could continue their journey to the Promised Land of Canaan, Rickett continued, "God gave His children a test. The test was twofold: would they receive His word and would they follow His anointed leader?"

"For months now, there has been a concerted effort to undermine the growth of our church. There have been members of this body refusing to attend the church services and refusing to contribute, with either their time or money, to the work God has laid before us.

"I'm not talking about the homebound or those who are not physically well. I'm talking about those who are spiritually sick and determined to stay that way."

"This church has been given a mission to accomplish – and the Lord has given us His word as the roadmap to follow."

Rickett drew in his breath and stepped to the side of the pulpit, and with tears beginning to form in his eyes, he recounted how he had been called to be their pastor;

how he had led them through the building program; how he "ran herd" on the vendors, the subcontractors, and yes, even the contractor, Lucas Marcum. Without his energy and oversight, the church would probably not be finished today. And the cost, yes the cost, would have been astronomical had he not personally intervened.

He continued. "Yet in spite of my efforts, pain, worry – and oh, yes, my prayers for guidance – there are those sitting among us tonight who defame my labor, and my name. It's not my labor or my name that is at issue here tonight. God called me to be your pastor, and you heard His call by extending to me this high office."

"The Apostle Paul worried that the good fruit of a church can and will be choked out by the thorns and thistles of dissension. In fact, he instructed the church at Corinth to separate themselves from those people. Cast them out, he urged. Yes, cast them out, lest the whole vine be destroyed."

"Just as Moses was anointed by God to lead His children to the Promised Land, God has also planted me, your humble servant. This is a tremendous task. There can only be one leader. A house divided against itself cannot stand."

Emotions began to rise in the congregation, and the few sounds of "Amen" that sprinkled his sermon began to mount into a crescendo of emotional agreement. As Rickett continued to preach, he no longer stood in place, but began to pace back and forth behind the pulpit, then down the steps, only to return to the pulpit with a finger pointing, or his head shaking in disgust, all of it orchestrated and directed for the benefit of everyone in attendance.

For those who worshipped Rickett, he was truly God's anointed. He had obviously been blasphemed by the unrepentant.

For those toward whom he had directed his message, he was obviously out of control, if not out of his mind. What in God's name was he talking about?

As Rickett concluded his message, he entertained a motion from the chairman of the deacon board. Ken Rowling rose to his feet, and with a typed message in his hand, read the following motion:

"It being evident that Two Springs is a constituted body of believers, united in spirit and in purpose to fulfill God's work in our city; and it being further evident that to fulfill that mission this church has appointed Dr. I.D. Rickett to be our leader and our pastor; and being made aware that neither our church nor our pastor will be able to accomplish the tasks set before them without the wholehearted support of each and every member here assembled, the deacon board does hereby move the church as follows:

All those who desire to remain in good standing with this body, and who pledge their support to Dr. Rickett as our pastor, please stand and say "Amen." To all those not in favor, please remain seated."

Everyone assembled knew exactly what was about to transpire. If you did not stand and say "Amen," you would be deemed a traitor to the cause of Christ. If you could not vote for the church and its pastor, you might as well resign your membership and leave the building.

But it really meant more than that. If you remained seated, you had just been expelled from membership. No need to wait for a resignation; no need to wait for you to leave; you were no longer a member of Two Springs Baptist Church and had no say whatsoever in would transpire thereafter.

The sneer on Rickett's face as he turned toward Lucas was malicious. "Got you!" he mouthed, as he pranced down the steps to greet his "sons of Levi." They gathered themselves together at the foot of the altar, almost dancing. It might as well have been the golden calf.

There was laughter and loud expressions of joy from the newer members of the church. Hugs, handshakes and pats on the back abounded as Lucas, his family, his friends and so many of the old Eleventh Street Church sat, dumbfounded and lifeless.

All those years of attending church, giving, praying, fellowshipping – yes loving and helping each other – and for what? Excommunication, and from a Baptist Church. Who would have ever dreamt it?

But it wasn't a dream. Forty-five members of Two Springs were instructed to leave the sanctuary, and to do so immediately, or the police would be called to escort them out. Indeed, two patrol cars were parked in front of the church with their emergency lights flashing. Rickett had called the chief of police with his concern about violence breaking out in the service, and he had requested some protection, just in case.

❖

Undeterred, Maggie was determined to shake Rickett's hand one more time. Tearfully, but still in control of her emotions, she dutifully got in line and slowly proceeded to the lobby where Rickett stood with his wife, both sons and two large men behind him. As Maggie approached and extended her right hand, Rickett looked aghast and quickly lowered his arm to his side. Maggie, innocently thinking he was still joking and acting the part of an innocent abuser, reached down for his hand to shake it.

That's when all hell broke loose at Two Springs. Rickett jumped back behind the two large men hired to be Rickett's bodyguards and accused Maggie of reaching for his manhood. He raised his voice so that all could hear his feeble cry for help. "My God, Maggie, what are you trying to do?" he shouted. "That's disgusting."

Thankfully, Lucas had taken his normal exit route out a side door, but soon realized something was amiss at the front. He ran, almost tripping over the parking lot curb, to the front porch where Maggie stood weeping, crouched over and nearly falling to her knees.

The police were dragging two of Lucas's nephews to their patrol car and proceeded to handcuff them in the presence of nearly the entire church. They had tried to defend Maggie's honor with fisticuffs thrown in Rickett's direction, and elbows to the gut of his two bodyguards. But Rickett now safely stood behind his wife, his eyes wildly aglow, pointing his finger and giving directions to his loyal clan to disperse, screaming that he would be fine, that they had done the right thing tonight. "Thank God," he cried. "The snakes have finally shed their skin and shown their true colors!"

Mark was still in the lobby standing next to Vernon Lawrence, a man who had been his Sunday school teacher. Mark had sat near Vernon in church for most of his teenage life. He adored Vernon, and did his best to imitate him in song. Vernon's bass voice, and the sounds of his deep and melodious vocals, were a marvel to Mark. Vernon had stood and said "Amen." Mark had not. They would never see or speak to each other again.

By week's end, Will Singleton had sought out and hired a lawyer. He sued the church and I.D. Rickett. The Hamilton Journal had a field day with the court pleadings, the interviews of the principal parties in the litigation, and the lawyers.

26.

Brother Against Brother

Will's role as plaintiff in the lawsuit soon expanded to others in the fray. All who had been excluded from church membership were collectively named as "the other plaintiffs." The lawsuit alleged that Rickett had executed and recorded a quitclaim deed, attempting to transfer the church property to the recently formed non-profit corporation, "Two Springs Baptist Church, Incorporated." Rickett had indeed transferred ownership of the property, which had previously been titled to the "Trustees" for the use and benefit of all the members. Behind all the legalese in the formal complaint was the plain and simple implication: "Rickett stole the property for his own gain and glory."

The other part of Singleton's complaint alleged that Rickett had no right under the church bylaws to excommunicate anyone except for conduct unbecoming a Christian. Merely disagreeing with the leadership of the church was not a sin worthy of exclusion, if a sin at all. The Bible should be the guide for wholesome conduct, not the personal likes or dislikes of any one person or group.

At the preliminary hearing, the Judge faced a serious quandary. Was the thrust of the lawsuit over property rights, or over theological doctrine? If over property rights, the Court might have jurisdiction over the dispute.

If over church doctrine, the Judge believed that any relief sought by Will Singleton and his fellow plaintiffs would be barred by the Court's own doctrine. That legal doctrine was explained by the Judge as the "doctrine of ecclesiastical abstention." In layman's terms, it meant that the Judge would not rule on disputes over religious theology.

Rickett's lawyer contended that the entire dispute involved church control and authority, both of which were based upon religious doctrine. As such, he argued, the Court had no jurisdiction in subject matter to interfere with the dispute.

However, the Judge concluded that judicial intervention was justified when it could be accomplished by resorting to neutral principle of law, and by doing so without consideration of doctrinal matters of worship or the tenets of faith. In other words, the Court would permit the lawsuit to continue as to the charge of an unlawful transfer of church property. That issue did not involve a consideration of the Church's doctrinal matters, only property law.

To do otherwise, the Judge said, would run the risk of placing a religious institution in a preferred position. By favoring the church over a secular institution, other constitutional concerns would arise, such as the Establishment Clause, where issues of separation of church and state issues would no doubt arise. As

Singleton's lawyer later explained, the Judge meant that even a preacher cannot steal from his own church.

The Singleton group rejoiced. They privately imagined how they would take back ownership of the church property, depriving Rickett of his earthly tabernacle. By forcing Rickett to deed the property back to the original trustees, they were confident his spirit would be broken, his pride quashed and his credentials as the "President" of the church incorporated irreparably destroyed.

But they were wrong. On the matter of excommunication, the Judge declined to interfere in the intra-church dispute. Rickett's lawyer argued that no one had actually been excluded or voted out of the church. Rather, he argued, the motion before the church body was only one of support for Rickett and the mission of the church. He continued by saying that the plaintiffs had failed to vote in favor of that support and voluntarily left the fellowship of the church.

He insisted that those in Singleton's group were not voted out of the church. They quit. Rickett's lawyer further alleged that the entire lawsuit before the Court was founded in anger and personal animus toward Dr. Rickett. He concluded by stating that the issue was one of church doctrine, ecclesiastical in nature, and that the Court should abstain from interfering. The Judge agreed.

So, after the preliminary hearing, both sides had reason to rejoice. The Singleton group could continue to press for a return of the church property from the corporation to the Trustees, but would have to remain as subjects of his lordship, Dr. I.D. Rickett. Singleton didn't like it and neither did Rickett.

The cost of litigation had already exceeded the financial resources of everyone involved, and as time passed, most everyone had taken an irrevocable stance. Rickett's congregation would not surrender the property without a fight, and the Singleton group vowed to never step foot on the property as long as Rickett remained.

Rickett's insatiable lust for power was equaled only by his incurable desire for praise. The "excluded ones," as they referred to themselves, were in no mood to be subjected to his power and would not utter a kind word in his direction.

Children of the "excluded ones" never fully recovered. Many stopped attending any church altogether, and forever after looked askance at anyone professing to be a minister. Those who did make a partial recovery from the spiritual drama bore scars of doubt in their fellow man for the rest of their life. They never fully trusted anyone again. Time may heal a wound, but scars last a lifetime.

After months of depositions, motions and delays, the matter was finally settled by an Agreed Order approved by the Court of Common Pleas of Butler County. The Agreed Order recited verbatim a motion unanimously passed by the body of Two Springs. It stated in part, that "Will Singleton and all other individuals who allegedly excluded themselves from membership by their vote, be reinstated as members of said church, and that they are hereby restored to their rights as members thereof."

The court's decision had no effect on the excluded members. No one ever returned. Lucas would never hear the message that Rickett preached in church the Sunday after, no doubt proclaiming victory and vindication for everything he did. No, Two Springs belonged to Rickett. The majority had chosen, and they had gathered around him. They were on the Lord's side. Rickett had been standing there all along, just waiting for them to come over.

Maggie didn't miss a beat. The next Sunday, she was in a church. She was not at Two Springs, but a church, any Baptist Church nearby. She visited Marvin and Shorty at Bordon Avenue. She visited Westside Baptist just down the road from home. She visited and visited until she finally settled on a church in which she felt at home.

Lucas didn't have the heart to visit another church, at least for a while. He knew so many people, and he feared that the conversation would eventually turn to Two Springs. He did his best not to think about the dastardly acts of Rickett, but they kept haunting him, following him at night along with the intermittent nightmares of war.

As with the war, Lucas would not speak of Two Springs, nor would he utter Rickett's name.

27.

Return to Eleventh Street

The following spring, while Maggie was attending her Wednesday church service, Lucas decided to drive around the city. He hoped to free his mind of worry about family, work and of course, Two Springs Baptist Church. Absentmindedly and without any intention of doing so, he found himself on East Avenue, near Eleventh Street. Not meaning to enter, he drove slowly down the same street he had traveled thousands of times, approaching the site of AME Zion Church.

He parked his truck on the street, near the alley, and sat with the truck windows lowered. He could hear the beautiful singing and shouts of praise inside. He looked at the front door, and remembered an older version of that same opening – and the night he surrendered his life to Jesus.

Perhaps for sentimental reasons, but maybe because of a burning desire to touch a familiar memory, he felt compelled to exit his truck and walk up to the porch. He stepped closer to the church. He reached for the door frame and touched it. He almost caressed the door as memories flooded back into his mind. Good memories; comforting memories. As he leaned against the door and began to kneel, an elderly black man opened the door.

"Welcome, brother," he said. "Come on in; got to hear the Reverend Stockton preach; this is going to be his last sermon."

Lucas quietly slipped into a seat in the back pew and sat down to listen to the first sermon he had heard in months. This sermon would be the Reverend's last in Eleventh Street. From his chair on the pulpit, the Reverend glanced toward the rear of the sanctuary. His eyes met those of Lucas.

Two men, different in so many ways, had been led by destiny to stand in the same ring of battle. Both with the face of a warrior, tough and intense, yet each casting a glow of meekness.

The Reverend Stockton struggled as he rose from his chair. He finally stood to his full height and carefully made his way to the pulpit, which seemed to shrink in size as the Reverend got closer and closer to it. His broad shoulders turned to face the congregation. With both of his huge, strong hands, he grasped each side of the pulpit to steady himself and slowly began to speak.

His voice was deep, melodious and magnetic. This was his last sermon at Eleventh Street. The Bible passage to which the Reverend directed everyone was familiar to Lucas. He remembered hearing the same scripture being read in this same building, so many years before. It had been the text of Pastor's farewell sermon as well.

It hadn't been chance or circumstance that brought the Reverend Stockton into Lucas's life. They had been engaged in the same fight, just in different corners of the ring. Lucas lowered his gaze as the Reverend reached the climatic conclusion to his sermon.

Lucas knew that the battles of life would continue, and he prayed that God would give him strength to finish the course, to keep the faith. He remembered the words of Shorty: "Press on, and forget those things which are behind."

The Reverend finished his sermon by saying, "May the grace of God be with you all." And all the church said, "Amen."

Without speaking to anyone, Lucas rose from his pew and walked out the same front door by which he had entered. He touched the doorframe one last time. He stood on the front porch and drew in a deep breath. He mumbled a verse of scripture that he had memorized so many years ago – the same verse Pastor had quoted the day Lucas joined the church:

"This is the day which the Lord hath made; we will rejoice and be glad in it."

Lucas walked to his truck. "Rejoice and be glad," he thought. "Indeed, that's what Pastor would say." As he started the engine, he realized that his story, his personal journey, would continue. He could not and would not forsake all that he knew to be true. He had truly learned that life was much more than survival; and that joy, though a distant cousin to peace, could be found. Then and only then would everything fall into place. At least for tonight, he was at peace.

About the Author

Steven K. Bowling was born in Hamilton, Ohio. He graduated *magna cum laude* from Carson-Newman College with a Bachelor of Science in 1971. In 1973, he became a Certified Public Accountant.

He received his J.D. with honors from the University of Tennessee College of Law in 1987. Prior to joining Howard & Howard, P.C., Mr. Bowling was the managing partner of the law firm of Shumate & Bowling in Knoxville. He focuses his practice in the areas of estate planning and probate matters, taxation and tax controversies for estate, business law for individuals and closely held businesses and general business planning.

Eleventh Street is his first novel.

51457427R00146

Made in the USA
San Bernardino, CA
22 July 2017